# TURBO DETECTIVE STORIES

## From East Los Angeles During the 1970's

### A Book of Fiction by Robert Nerbovig

Cover Art by Robert Nerbovig

solartoys@yahoo.com

# Prologue

The hot California sun baked the cracked asphalt of the East L.A. streets. Turbo wiped the sweat from his brow as he stepped out of his powder blue Chevy Corvette Convertible, which had been completely restored, after competing on the local drag strips, Irwindale and Pomona raceway.

Turbo a devoted car enthusiast, bought the corvette and completely restored it. It has a 500 Cu. Inch Moroso motor, 4″ bubble hood, 2″ dropped front end, new interior, new paint, Goodyear 60 tires, American Mags, and a 3000 RPM stall-speed on the torque converter.

Despite the 1970s being in full swing, the "barrios" hadn't changed much since the 50s.

Lowriders cruised the boulevards, hydraulics hitching up the rear wheels. As Chicano rap and funk rhythms filled

the air, creating a unique soundscape that resonated with the people on the street.

The tantalizing aroma filled the air from the street vendors and the open windows of shops selling tamales and raspadas. If you listened closely, you could almost hear the melancholy notes of oldies drifting up from backyard barbecues.

Turbo is about 5'8" with a muscular and athletic build, his ruggedly handsome face features striking brown eyes and a strong jawline, his hair is naturally dark brown, and is typically styled in a short, cropped cut. Turbo will often sport a light stubble or well-groomed beard.

As he stepped out of his car he straightened his leather jacket, his eyes sweeping across the familiar landscape. This was his turf - he knew where every pothole was, and how every graffiti tag

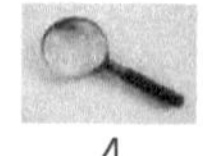

held a story. Those sleazy joints masquerading as respectable businesses, couldn't fool him. As a private eye in this gritty part of town, he encountered all sorts: from the Gangbangers, hustlers, and those housewives that were getting a little too friendly with the milkman.

He checked his surroundings once more before lighting up a lucky Strike. This was another day of solving cases and keeping the city's seedy underbelly in check. A slow smile crept across Turbo's face, let the fun begin he murmured as he flicked away the match. Let the fun begin.

Each case was different, a microcosm of
the simmering tensions of East LA. Turbo
navigated a world of suspicion, petty
crime, and misplaced dreams. His office
became a confessional booth, a stage for
the city's hidden stories. By the end of
the month, the tamales had been replaced
by a dented coffee pot, this change is a
concession to the endless nights spent
tailing philandering husbands, tracking
down stolen guitars, and searching for a
runaway daughter.

## Saving the Family Ranch

A new client appeared at the door, *Cat Cordero he was a grizzled old man with a weathered face and wearing a worn old black cowboy hat.*

*Like a story reminiscent of the old West, he sat down, and his story began to unfold like a forgotten Western. His ranch, the heart of his family for generations, was under threat from Blake Morgan a Developer, known for seeking inexpensive land, and posed a threat to the ranch that had been the heart of his family for generations, nestled in a valley untouched by the city's sprawl,* was under threat from a ruthless developer with a taste for cheap land.

Turbo looked at the man, another victim of a city constantly pushing its boundaries, and a weary sigh escaped his lips. He knew what he had to do.

The grizzled rancher, Cat Cordero he was a grizzled old man with a weathered face and wearing a worn old black cowboy hat.

Like a story reminiscent of the old West, he sat down, and his story began to unfold,

Cat, sat across from Turbo, his weathered face etched with worry. His ranch, the heart of his family for generations, was under threat from Blake Morgan a Developer, known for seeking inexpensive land, and posed a threat to the ranch that had been the heart of his family for generations, nestled in a valley untouched by the city's sprawl. Turbo looked at the man, another victim of a city constantly pushing its boundaries, *and* a weary sigh escaped his lips. He knew what he had to do.

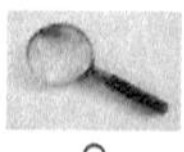

Morgan, a man with a shark-like grin and a reputation for dirty tactics, offered a pittance for the land, a sum that barely covered the property taxes.

The days seemed to stretch endlessly, the heat causing the asphalt to shimmer like a mirage.

*This case was different.*

It wasn't about stolen goods or missing persons. It was about a fight for a way of life, a battle against the relentless tide of progress that threatened to swallow whole the quiet dignity of Mr. Cordero's ranch. A flicker of something akin to nostalgia flickered in Turbo's eyes, Turbo understood the rancher's attachment to the land, the deep-rooted connection *transcending* mere ownership.

*The days seemed to stretch endlessly, the heat causing the asphalt to shimmer like a mirage.*

Turbo, ever the resourceful investigator, dug into Morgan's past, He discovered a trail of broken promises and dubious land deals, a pattern of exploiting legal loopholes and intimidating landowners.

The rancher, despite his calloused hands and quiet demeanor, possessed a fierce determination to protect his heritage.

A breakthrough came from an unlikely source - a disgruntled ex-employee of Morgan's, a woman named Velia who felt cheated out of her fair share in a previous land deal. Velia, fueled by a desire for revenge and a sense of justice, shared incriminating documents that exposed Morgan's plan to exploit a hidden mineral deposit on the Cordero ranch.

Armed with this information, Turbo and Cat Cordero approached the local environmental commission. They presented

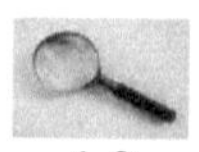

a compelling case, highlighting the ecological significance of the untouched valley and the potential damage Morgan's development plans could wreak. The rancher's passionate plea, combined with Velia's damning evidence, swayed the commission. An injunction was placed on the development, putting a temporary halt to Morgan's bulldozers.

Cat Cordero, with a grateful nod and a calloused hand extended in thanks, bid Turbo farewell. The victory felt significant, a small win against the forces of unchecked greed. Yet, Turbo knew the fight wasn't over. Morgan, a man with a vindictive streak, wouldn't go down easily.

## The Missing Mural

A new client, a nervous young woman named Margaret, walked into Turbo's office. Her story, a tale of a missing mural and a

threatened cultural center in the heart of East LA, felt like a familiar echo. The mural, a vibrant tapestry depicting the history of the Latino community, was more than just art; it was a symbol of their resilience and identity. A wealthy developer, with plans for a luxury condo complex, intended to demolish the cultural center, erasing the mural and a vital piece of the community's soul.

Turbo looked at Margaret, her eyes burning with a fierce pride, and a familiar weariness settled over him. But then, a spark of determination ignited in his own eyes. The city may never truly rest, but neither would he. He was Turbo, and this was his city. And as long as there were shadows threatening to engulf the light, he would be there, a solitary figure in a worn fedora, ready to face them, one case at a time.

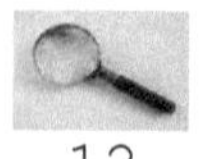

Smoke tendrils rose from a crumpled pack of cigarettes on the desk, beside a faded flyer depicting the missing mural - a vibrant explosion of colors depicting generations of Latino families weaving through the city's history. Margaret, the young woman who'd brought the case, sat across from him, her fire tempered by anxiety.

"They say it's progress, Mr. Turbo," she said, her voice laced with anger and despair. "But what progress is it that erases our stories?"

Turbo, the lines on his face etched deeper by the relentless parade of East LA's struggles, understood. This wasn't just about bricks and mortar. This was a fight for identity, for a community's right to its own narrative.

Following a trail of rumors and whispers, Turbo found himself in the polished office of the developer, a man named

Parker Thorne. Thorne, with his manicured nails and condescending smile, embodied everything the community feared. He saw the cultural center and the mural as mere inconveniences, disposable relics of a bygone era.

The investigation took a detour when a local artist named Mondo, known for his graffiti murals depicting the city's soul, came to Turbo with a tip. He'd overheard a conversation at a swanky bar about a "relocation project." Apparently, Thorne wasn't just planning to demolish the cultural center; he intended to "salvage" the mural - a euphemism that sent shivers down Turbo's spine.

He connected the dots - Thorne planned to dismantle the mural, break it into pieces, and sell them off at a premium to wealthy art collectors, erasing its significance in the process.

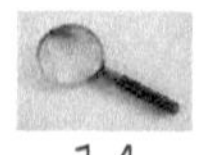

With time running out and fueled by a righteous anger, Turbo devised a plan. He enlisted Mondo and a ragtag crew of local artists, their brushes and spray cans their weapons. He rallied the community, their voices rising in a chorus of protest. Social media, a new and powerful tool, amplified their cause.

The day of Thorne's demolition crew arrival dawned tense. Yet, instead of a bulldozer, a sea of protestors greeted them. Local journalists, alerted by the social media frenzy, documented the spectacle. The cameras flashed, capturing the anger and the unity of the community. The police, caught in the crossfire, were forced to delay the demolition.

The fight extended to the city council chambers, a battle fought with words and passionate pleas. Margaret, her voice trembling but strong, spoke of the

mural's significance, of the stories it held, the history it documented. Mondo, with a poet's eloquence, spoke of art as a heartbeat of a community. Against the odds, public pressure swayed the council. A preservation order was passed, a temporary victory for the cultural center and the mural.

A tired but triumphant Margaret offered Turbo a warm embrace, a silent acknowledgement of their shared fight. The community, energized by their success, rallied around the cultural center, organizing fundraising events and volunteering their time to refurbish the building.

### Rival Gangs

A new client walked in, a young man named Bobby, his eyes filled with a desperate hope. His brother, Georgie, a talented musician who'd helped Turbo in a previous

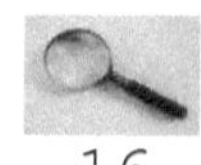

case, had gone missing after a run-in with a notorious gang leader.

Turbo, with a sigh that mirrored the city's perpetual churn, accepted the case. He knew what he had to do. As he looked out his window, the relentless sunshine glinted off the vibrant colors of the saved mural, a testament to the community's spirit. It was a small victory, a fleeting moment of peace, before the city's relentless rhythm pulled him back into the fray. He was Turbo, and this was his city. And as long as the shadows lurked, he would be there, a solitary figure in a worn fedora, ready to face them, one case, one fight for justice, at a time.

The air hung heavy with the smell of desperation and simmering tension. Inside Turbo's office, the air conditioner wheezed its last, offering little respite from the relentless sun.

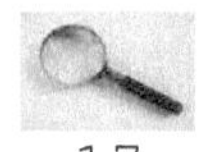

Bobby, the young man seeking his brother, Georgie, sat across from him, worry etched on his youthful face. Bobby, the talented musician who'd helped in the case against the veterans' home drug ring, had vanished without a trace after a heated confrontation with Eddie "El Serpiente" Ramirez, leader of the notorious Calle Serpiente gang.

This was different. This wasn't a missing person or a petty theft. This was a tangled web of gang loyalty, territorial disputes, and a power struggle that threatened to erupt into violence. Turbo felt a knot tighten in his stomach. He knew the dangers of delving into the underbelly of gang warfare, but Bobby's desperation mirrored the city's own yearning for a semblance of peace. With a heavy sigh, Turbo accepted the case.

The following days were a blur of dead ends and cryptic warnings. Turbo

revisited the scene of the argument, a dingy bar frequented by lowlifes and fringe gang members. He spent nights trawling the city's underbelly, a lone wolf amidst a pack of snarling predators. He talked to anyone who knew Georgie - fellow musicians, barflies, even a disillusioned ex-gang member who confided in a whispered conversation over greasy diner coffee. Each interaction chipped away at Turbo's optimism, revealing a city fractured by violence, fueled by a desperate search for power and respect.

August arrived, bringing with it the annual Calle Serpiente block party, a dubious celebration of the gang's dominance. Turbo, disguised in a worn leather jacket and a baseball cap pulled low, navigated the throng of bodies, a silent observer amidst the cacophony of music and bravado. He spotted El

Serpiente, a charismatic but cold-eyed young man radiating a dangerous aura. Every fiber of Turbo's being screamed caution, but he knew this was his only chance to gather information, even if it meant walking into the lion's den.

He approached El Serpiente under the guise of seeking a lost friend who, coincidentally, resembled Georgie. The gang leader's eyes narrowed, but something about Turbo's weathered face and quiet demeanor seemed to disarm him. In a tense exchange, El Serpiente admitted to a confrontation with Georgie but denied any knowledge of his whereabouts. A flicker of doubt crossed El Serpiente's face, however, a hint that something more sinister might be at play. A breakthrough came from an unexpected source — a young woman named Cece, an aspiring journalist who frequented the same diner as Turbo. Cece, fueled by a

desire for truth and a fierce loyalty to her neighborhood, revealed she'd overheard a conversation between two Calle Serpiente members mentioning a rival gang, Gymtown, and a "debt to be settled."

Following this lead, Turbo, with Cece as his reluctant partner, ventured into the heart of Gymtown territory. The streets were tense, every glance a potential threat. They found their target - a wiry man with a scarred face and a menacing glint in his eyes known as "El Diablo." Under the duress of a well-placed threat and a surprising assist from Cece's quick wit, El Diablo revealed a shocking truth: Gymtown had lured Georgie into their territory, mistaking him for a rival gang member.

Armed with this information, Turbo, El Serpiente (reluctantly drawn into a precarious alliance), and Cece stormed a

derelict warehouse on the city's outskirts, the suspected location of Georgie's captivity. The ensuing confrontation was a blur of adrenaline and violence. Fists flew, gunshots echoed in the cavernous space. Through it all, Turbo pushed forward, a relentless force fueled by a desperate hope.

He found Georgie, dazed and injured, but alive. Relief washed over Turbo, a fleeting moment of victory amidst the chaos. El Serpiente, forced to confront the repercussions of his gang's actions, agreed to a truce with Gymtown, a fragile peace brokered by the unlikely alliance. Cece, her journalistic instincts kicking in, captured the entire confrontation on her camera, a story that promised to expose the city's brutal gang wars.

The truce brokered by Turbo held, a testament to the precarious balance of power in the city's underworld. Georgie,

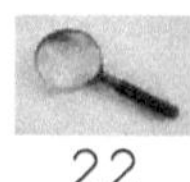

physically and emotionally scarred, reunited with his teary-eyed brother Bobby. El Serpiente, his charisma dimmed by a newfound vulnerability, offered a curt nod of respect to Turbo in a silent acknowledgement of his role in the events.

## A Botanist Gone Missing

A frantic young woman named Mary burst into Turbo's office, her eyes wide with terror. Her father, a renowned botanist named Dr. Loya, had vanished from his research lab at a local university. Dr. Loya, a man dedicated to preserving the city's dwindling native plant life, was on the cusp of a breakthrough – a drought-resistant strain of wildflowers that could revitalize barren patches of the city.

This case felt different. It wasn't about violence or gang warfare. It was a race

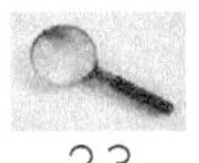

against time, a desperate search for a man whose life's work held the potential to breathe life back into a parched city. A flicker of something akin to admiration ignited in Turbo's eyes. He admired Dr. Loya's dedication, his quiet determination to make a difference, one seed at a time.

The following days were a whirlwind of activity. Turbo delved into Dr. Loya's research, deciphering cryptic notes and botanical diagrams. He interviewed colleagues, their faces etched with a mixture of concern and confusion. A security guard at the university mentioned a heated argument Dr. Loya had with a representative of a large landscaping corporation known for its ruthless tactics.

Following the trail of the landscaping corporation, Turbo found himself confronting a slick executive named Mr.

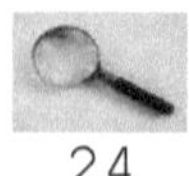

Ortiz. Ortiz, a man with a steely glint in his eyes and a smile that didn't reach them, dismissed Dr. Loya's research as "quaint" and "unprofitable." However, a flicker of something akin to fear crossed Thornton's face when Turbo mentioned the drought-resistant wildflowers.

Then, a breakthrough came from an unlikely source - a group of student environmental activists who frequented the same diner as Turbo. They revealed whispers about a clandestine meeting between Ortiz's representatives and a notorious group of land developers known for their blatant disregard for environmental concerns.

Turbo, armed with this information, infiltrated the clandestine meeting, a tense gathering held in a secluded room within a luxurious hotel. He listened as Ortiz and the developers discussed a lucrative plan to develop a vast swathe

of public land, a plan that hinged on discrediting Dr. Loya's research and suppressing the existence of the drought-resistant wildflowers.

With the incriminating evidence from the meeting, Turbo exposed Ortiz's plan to the university administration and the local media. Public outrage erupted. The university, facing mounting pressure, launched a search for Dr. Loya, mobilizing resources previously unavailable to Turbo.

A frantic call from the university security guard cut through the quiet. They had found Dr. Loya, held captive in a remote greenhouse owned by the landscaping corporation, his research notes stolen. Dr. Loya, weak but resolute, revealed he had been abducted in an attempt to silence him.

Turbo, fueled by a combination of anger and determination, led a police raid on

the greenhouse. They found Dr. Loya's stolen research notes, along with evidence linking the landscaping corporation to the abduction. Ortiz, his carefully constructed facade crumbling, was apprehended.

Dr. Loya, recovering in the hospital, received a visit from a grateful university president. The university, vowing to learn from their mistakes, pledged to support Dr. Loya's research and promote sustainable landscaping practices. The media, captivated by the tale of the missing botanist and his drought-resistant wildflowers, painted Dr. Loya as a hero, a champion for the city's fragile ecosystem.

Turbo, sitting in his office, the whirring of a newly installed fan a welcome relief from the heat, pondered the city's complexities. He had seen its darkness and despair, the brutal

underbelly that thrived in the shadows. But he had also witnessed acts of courage, of resilience, a community's unwavering spirit that refused to be extinguished. He was just a solitary figure in a worn fedora, but maybe, just maybe, he had made a difference.

## The Missing Muralist

As the relentless California sun dipped below the horizon, casting long shadows across his office, a new knock on the door shattered the silence. A young woman with worry etched on her face stood before him. Her story, a tale of a missing muralist and a threatened community garden in the heart of East LA, felt chillingly familiar. Yet, despite the weariness in his bones, a flicker ...of determination ignited in Turbo's eyes. The city may never truly rest, but neither would he. He was Turbo, and this

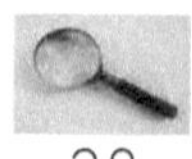

was his city. And as long as shadows threatened to engulf the light, he would be there, a solitary figure in a worn fedora, ready to face them, one case, one fight for justice, at a time.

This new client, Celina, explained her concern for Anthony, a renowned muralist known for his vibrant depictions of the city's cultural tapestry. Anthony had vanished without a trace after a heated argument with the owner of a local construction company, Mr. Harris. Harris, a man with a reputation for ruthless development projects, planned to build a luxury condominium complex on the very plot where Peter intended to create his most ambitious mural yet - a sprawling testament to the spirit of East LA.

This case resonated with Turbo. It wasn't just about a missing artist or a threatened artwork. It was a battle for

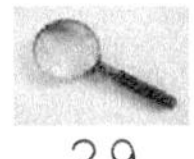

the soul of the city, a fight against the relentless tide of gentrification that threatened to erase the vibrant history and cultural identity of East LA. A spark of defiance flickered in Turbo's weathered face. He wouldn't let another piece of the city's heart be ripped away. The following days were a blur of activity. Turbo tracked down Anthony's last known location - a dusty abandoned warehouse on the outskirts of the city. The warehouse, rumored to be a temporary holding ground for displaced residents facing eviction by Mr. Harris' company, yielded no clues of Anthony's whereabouts. However, whispers from a wary caretaker revealed Harris' penchant for strong-arm tactics and his disdain for anything that stood in the way of his development plans.

September arrived, the Santa Ana winds whipping sand across the parched

landscape. A glimmer of hope surfaced from an unexpected source - a group of street artists, Anthony's friends and admirers. They revealed a hidden message Anthony had left behind in one of his unfinished murals - a cryptic symbol that pointed towards a local community center known for its activism against gentrification.

At the community center, Turbo met a passionate young organizer named Karen. Karen, armed with knowledge of the city's intricate network of activists, informed him about a planned protest against Harris' demolition crew scheduled for the following day. She believed Anthony might be involved, using his artistic talents to support the cause.

Turbo joined the protest, a sea of determined faces chanting slogans against displacement and the erasure of cultural heritage. He spotted Anthony not

as a captive, but as a participant - his paint-splattered hands wielding a brush in a feverish display of artistic defiance.

The protest escalated as Harris' demolition crew arrived. A tense standoff ensued, the crowd holding their ground against the rumbling bulldozers. Then, a flicker of movement caught Turbo's eye. A group of men in black suits, hired muscle employed by Harris, were attempting to snatch Anthony away from the crowd.

Adrenaline surged through Turbo. In a blur of fists and grit, he fought his way through the throng, determined to protect Anthony. The ensuing scuffle was a chaotic dance of desperation and resilience. Just as it seemed the men in black would overpower them, a deafening roar filled the air.

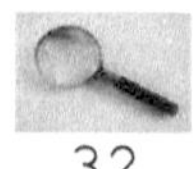

A fire engine, alerted by the commotion, screeched to a halt, its sirens wailing. The firemen, witnessing the struggle, intervened, forming a human barricade between Anthony and his captors. The police, finally arriving on the scene, apprehended Harris' men, their faces contorted in a mixture of anger and frustration.

Anthony, shaken but free, stood with Turbo amidst the crowd of cheering protestors. Harris' demolition plans were put on hold, a temporary victory for the community and its vibrant artistic spirit. Karen, with a grateful smile, offered Turbo a handshake, acknowledging his role in the fight.

As the last rays of the setting sun painted the sky in hues of orange and pink, Turbo felt a familiar weariness settle over him. Yet, a sense of quiet satisfaction lingered. He may be just one

man, but he had stood with the community, a silent guardian against the forces that threatened to devour its soul. The city, with its ever-present shadows and struggles, would continue its relentless hum. But for now, in this small corner of East LA, a flicker of hope had been ignited, a testament to the enduring spirit of its people and the power of art to fight for a brighter future.

Turbo, with a sigh that mirrored the city's perpetual churn, looked out his window. The vibrant colors of a newly completed mural, depicting the triumph of the community garden protest, shimmered in the fading light. It was a small victory, a fleeting moment of peace.

A worn photograph on Turbo's desk depicted a smiling young woman with fiery red hair – Celina, the artist who'd ignited the fight for the community garden.

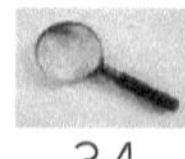

## The Family Farm is Under Attack

A new client sat across from him, a man with calloused hands and a worried frown etched deep into his weathered face.

"Mr. Turbo," the man rasped, his voice thick with a rural accent, "they say you're the one to see when trouble comes knockin'."

Turbo leaned back in his creaking chair, the faint ache in his lower back a constant reminder of past battles. "Trouble comes knockin' a lot around here," he said, his voice gravelly with years of wear and tear.

The man introduced himself as Mario, a farmer from a small town on the outskirts of the city. His family's land, a fertile patch nurtured by generations, was under threat from a powerful corporation named Agron, Inc. Agron, notorious for its ruthless land acquisition practices, intended to convert Mario's farm into a

35

massive industrial complex, a concrete jungle swallowing up the lifeblood of the land.

This case felt different. It wasn't about the city's underbelly or artistic battles. It was a fight for a way of life, a desperate plea to preserve a legacy carved from sweat and sunbaked soil. A flicker of something akin to nostalgia flickered in Turbo's eyes. He understood Mario's attachment to the land, the deep-rooted connection that transcended mere ownership. It was a connection he himself yearned for, a yearning for a simpler time, a time before the city's relentless sprawl had devoured everything in its path.

Following a trail of broken promises and dubious land deals, Turbo found himself face-to-face with the polished veneer of Agron's headquarters. Mr. Henderson, the CEO, a man with a steely gaze and a

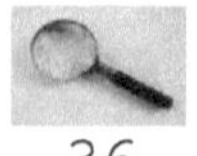

predatory smile, dismissed Mario's concerns with a practiced ease. He spoke of "progress" and "economic development," words that rang hollow in the sterile confines of the corporate office.

The investigation took a detour when a disgruntled former employee of Agron, a young woman named Carol with a rebellious streak, approached Turbo. Carol, disillusioned by the corporation's callous disregard for the environment, revealed incriminating documents that exposed Agron's plan to exploit a hidden aquifer beneath Mario's land, a water source vital for the entire region.

Turbo connected the dots – Agron wasn't just interested in the land; they coveted the hidden water source, a resource they intended to exploit for profit, leaving the surrounding communities parched and desperate.

With time running out and fueled by a righteous anger on behalf of Mario and countless others like him, Turbo devised a multi-pronged plan. He enlisted the help of a local environmental lawyer, a sharp woman named Susie who fought for the voiceless with unwavering tenacity. He contacted a team of investigative journalists, their cameras and microphones weapons in the fight for truth. He rallied the local community, farmers from neighboring towns joining Mario in a show of solidarity. Social media, now a powerful force for change, amplified their cause.

The day of Agron's construction crew arrival dawned tense. Yet, instead of bulldozers, a sea of protestors greeted them, a sea of faces etched with determination and a deep love for the land. News cameras flashed, capturing the passionate pleas of Mario, Susie's

scathing indictment of Agron's practices, and the unwavering resolve of the community. The pressure mounted, forcing Agron to temporarily halt construction.

The fight extended to the courtrooms, a battle fought with legal arguments and irrefutable evidence. Susie, a master strategist, presented carol's leaked documents and exposed Agron's deceptive environmental impact assessments. Public outcry intensified, fueled by the relentless media coverage. The judge, swayed by the weight of evidence and the sheer force of public opinion, issued a temporary injunction on the project.

A weary but triumphant Mario, tears glistening in his eyes, offered Turbo a calloused hand in gratitude. The community, energized by their success, organized fundraising events to support the legal battle against Agron. A sense

of hope, fragile but persistent, bloomed in the hearts of the people.

## Keeping Olvera Street Original

A nervous young woman named Mary, a graduate student studying urban planning, burst into Turbo's office. Her eyes, wide with fear, mirrored the tremor in her voice as she spoke of a looming threat to the very heart of LA - the historic Olvera Street.

Olvera Street, a vibrant marketplace pulsating with the city's rich Mexican heritage, was facing demolition plans from a newly formed development group called Oasis Rejuvenation. Oasis Rejuvenation, spearheaded by a charismatic businessman named Daniel Vargas, promised a luxurious mall complex, complete with high-end stores and sterile uniformity. They painted a picture of progress, economic

prosperity, and a sanitized version of East LA's cultural identity.

This case struck a deep chord within Turbo. Olvera Street wasn't just a marketplace; it was a living tapestry woven from generations of stories, a testament to the city's vibrant cultural heritage. He saw the glint of dollar signs in Vargas' eyes, a desire to erase the very essence of what made East LA unique in favor of a homogenized, profit-driven vision. A flicker of defiance ignited in his weathered face. He wouldn't let another piece of the city's soul be bulldozed into oblivion.

The following days were a whirlwind of activity. Turbo delved into the murky background of Oasis Rejuvenation, uncovering a web of political connections and questionable financial dealings. He spent nights interviewing shop owners on Olvera Street, their voices a chorus of

fear and determination. An elderly woman, her hands gnarled with age, spoke of her family business, a small shop selling handcrafted pottery, passed down through generations. A young artist, his passion evident in his vibrant paintings, spoke of the street as his canvas, a platform for his cultural expression. Each story resonated with Turbo, a testament to the irreplaceable value of Olvera Street.

A glimmer of hope surfaced from an unlikely source - a group of passionate history students from a local university. Led by a tenacious young professor named Dr. Valdez, the students had meticulously documented the historical significance of every building on Olvera Street. Their research, a treasure trove of information, became a crucial weapon in Turbo's arsenal.

Turbo, with Mary and Dr. Valdez by his side, held a community meeting at the

heart of Olvera Street. The energy was electric as shop owners, artists, historians, and everyday citizens shared their stories, painting a vivid picture of the street's cultural significance. Local media, captivated by the passionate outpouring, broadcasted the stories far and wide.

The students' research, combined with public pressure, forced the city council to hold a hearing on the Olvera Street development plans. The hearing room was packed, a sea of faces determined to protect their heritage. Turbo, Mary by his side once again, presented a compelling case, highlighting the historical significance of the street, the economic benefits of small businesses, and the intangible value of cultural identity. Dr. Valdez followed, his students presenting their meticulous documentation as evidence.

The council chambers buzzed with tension. Vargas, his facade of charm faltering under the weight of public scrutiny, delivered a slick presentation filled with empty promises and sanitized visions. Yet, the tide had turned. The council members, swayed by the overwhelming public sentiment and the undeniable evidence, voted to reject Oasis Rejuvenation's plans for Olvera Street.

A celebratory gathering erupted on Olvera Street, a joyous cacophony of music, laughter, and heartfelt speeches. Mary, beaming with relief, presented Turbo with a plaque handcrafted by a local artisan, a small token of immense gratitude. The shop owners, their eyes shining with newfound hope, vowed to work together to revitalize the street.

## The Missing Teacher

A knock on the door shattered the silence. A young man with a haunted look in his eyes stood before him. His story, a tale of a missing teacher and a suspected drug ring operating within a local high school, felt chillingly familiar. Despite the weariness in his bones, a flicker of determination ignited in Turbo's eyes. He was Turbo, and this was his city and as long as shadows threatened to engulf the light, he would be there, a solitary figure in a worn fedora, ready to face them, one case at a time.

The young man, his name was Trent, explained his concerns about Mr. Lopez, a charismatic and dedicated history teacher who had vanished without a trace. Mr. Lopez, known for his unconventional yet inspiring teaching methods, often took his students on impromptu tours of

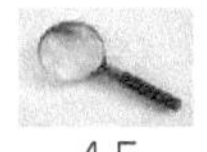

East LA's historical landmarks, including Olvera Street. Trent, one of Mr. Lopez's most devoted students, felt an unsettling dissonance in the teacher's disappearance.

This case felt different. It wasn't about land grabs or ruthless corporations. It was about the future of the city's youth, the potential corruption festering within the very institutions meant to nurture them. A knot of worry tightened in Turbo's gut. He knew the dark underbelly of the city stretched its tendrils into unexpected places, and the thought of it infiltrating a high school filled him with a cold dread.

The days stretched into February, a month with a deceptive air of calm that masked the city's underlying turmoil. Following a trail of hushed whispers and nervous glances among students, Turbo found himself navigating the labyrinthine

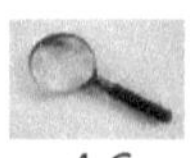

corridors of East LA High. The once
vibrant murals adorning the walls now
seemed faded, reflecting a sense of
neglect mirroring Mr. Lopez's
unexplained absence.

His investigation led him to a
disgruntled janitor, a man named Paco
tired of turning a blind eye to the
after-school activities in a particular
unused classroom. Paco revealed hushed
conversations about "product" and
"territory," words that sent a shiver
down Turbo's spine. He suspected a drug
ring operating within the school's walls,
a chilling prospect that could explain
Mr. Lopez's disappearance - perhaps he
stumbled upon their operation and became
a liability.

A glimmer of hope, faint yet persistent,
came from an unexpected source - a group
of tech-savvy students, Trent among them.
Inspired by Turbo's relentless pursuit of

the truth, they had discreetly hacked into the school's security system. One grainy video clip captured a late-night meeting in the unused classroom, revealing a group of individuals, their faces obscured by shadows, engaged in a tense exchange.

Turbo, armed with the video clip and fueled by a righteous anger, confronted the school principal, a stern woman named Ms. Rodriguez. Initially dismissive, her demeanor shifted upon witnessing the video. Ms. Rodriguez, a firm believer in education as a path out of poverty, revealed a history of complaints about suspicious activity near the unused classroom, complaints that had been ignored due to a lack of concrete evidence.

With renewed urgency, Turbo and Ms. Rodriguez collaborated. He shared his suspicions about a drug ring, while she

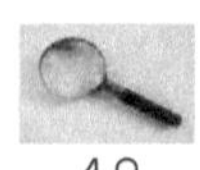

mobilized the school security team, discreetly deploying them near the unused classroom at night. Their gamble paid off. One moonlit night, the security team apprehended a group of individuals attempting to enter the classroom, their backpacks bulging with suspicious packages.

The apprehended individuals, connected to a notorious local gang, confessed to operating a drug ring within the school. Mr. Lopez, held captive to prevent him from exposing them, was located in a dilapidated warehouse on the city's outskirts. He was weak but alive, his spirit unbroken.

Mr. Lopez, his ordeal leaving a deep mark, decided to take a leave of absence to recover. However, his dedication to education remained undimmed. He pledged to work with Ms. Rodriguez to implement stricter security measures and establish

a confidential reporting system for students witnessing suspicious activity. A simple ceremony was held in the school auditorium, a celebration of Mr. Lopez's safe return and Ms. Rodriguez's swift action. Trent, beaming with pride, presented Turbo with a hand-drawn card signed by his classmates, a small gesture of immense gratitude. The students, their faces filled with a newfound sense of empowerment, erupted in cheers. As Turbo looked out at the sea of young faces, he saw a flicker of defiance in their eyes, a spark of resilience that promised a brighter future for their school, their community, and their city.

**Run Run Run Run Runaway**

The peace was shattered by the frantic knocking on his office door.
A woman, her face etched with worry lines deeper than any Turbo had seen before,

stood on the threshold. She introduced herself as Abbie, a social worker at a local homeless shelter. Her voice trembled as she spoke of a missing resident, a young woman named Heather, known for her vibrant spirit and artistic talent. Heather, a runaway struggling with addiction, had found a semblance of stability at the shelter. But she had vanished without a trace, leaving behind only a cryptic sketch depicting a desolate abandoned building on the city's forgotten outskirts.

This case gnawed at Turbo. It wasn't just about a missing person; it was a glimpse into the city's underbelly, the invisible population whose struggles often went unnoticed. Heather, a young woman with a bright spark dimmed by circumstance, deserved a chance. A flicker of compassion, mingled with a familiar determination, ignited in his eyes. He

wouldn't let Heather become another statistic another lost soul swallowed by the city's unforgiving streets.

The following days were a blur of activity. Turbo, fueled by a sense of urgency, delved into the city's forgotten corners, following the trail of Heather's sketch. He navigated through derelict alleyways and crumbling warehouses, the oppressive silence broken only by the relentless echo of his footsteps. He questioned wary locals, their faces etched with suspicion and indifference. Hope dwindled with each dead end, replaced by a gnawing fear that Heather might have met a tragic fate.

A street artist with a network of contacts in the city's homeless community, a young man named Dax with paint-splattered hands and a kind smile, informed Turbo about a group of runaways who frequented an abandoned subway

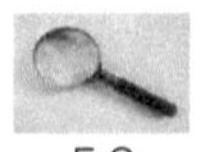

station rumored to be a haven for those on the fringes.

Turbo, armed with Dax's information and a cautious optimism, ventured into the dank darkness of the abandoned subway station. The air hung heavy with the smell of mildew and desperation. He navigated through graffiti-covered tunnels, the silence broken only by the dripping of water and the scurrying of unseen creatures.

Deep within the station's bowels, he stumbled upon a makeshift encampment inhabited by a group of weary teenagers. Heather was among them, her vibrant spirit dimmed but not extinguished. They revealed a chilling story of a predatory network that exploited runaways, luring them with promises of help before pushing them into a life of crime and addiction. With the help of Abbie, Turbo contacted the police and social services. A sting

operation was meticulously planned, with Dax discreetly informing the runaways about a safe haven at the homeless shelter. As Heather and others entered the designated building, undercover officers apprehended their captors. Heather, along with the other rescued runaways, received counseling and support at the shelter. Abbie, her eyes filled with gratitude, expressed her belief that with the right help, Heather could reclaim her life. Turbo, despite the weariness in his bones, felt a quiet satisfaction. He couldn't solve every problem, but he had made a difference, however small, in the lives of these vulnerable young people.

**Neon City's Ghost**

A young man with a nervous energy about him paced across the threadbare rug. He introduced himself as Andre, a computer

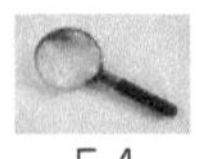

science student at UCLA with a story that
sent shivers down Turbo's spine.

"It's about a game, Mr. Ravelli," Andre
stammered, his voice barely above a
whisper. "A video game called 'Neon
City.'"

Video games, a rapidly growing form of
entertainment, weren't usually Turbo's
domain. But Andre's urgency, the tremor
in his voice, demanded attention. As
Andre explained, Neon City wasn't your
typical arcade game. It was a hyper-
realistic simulation eerily mimicking
East LA, a digital replica down to the
graffiti-laden alleyways and the
flickering neon signs. But there was a
sinister twist - the game mirrored real-
life events, even predicting them with
unsettling accuracy.

This case felt different. It wasn't about
gangs or missing persons. It was about a
possible breach of reality, a game

blurring the lines between simulation and the harsh streets of East LA. A seed of unease sprouted in Turbo's gut. Was this a harmless coincidence, or was something more sinister at play?

The following days were a blur of research and late-night discussions. Turbo delved into the murky world of video game development, a realm filled with passionate creators and cutthroat competition. He contacted the developers of Neon City, a reclusive company called Arcadia Interactive shrouded in secrecy. Their enigmatic CEO, a tech mogul named Alistair Thorne, refused to meet, dismissing Andre's concerns as "hysteria."

A breakthrough came from an unlikely source - a group of tech-savvy teenagers who frequented the same diner as Turbo. They were avid gamers, their faces

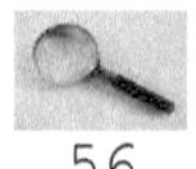

illuminated by the glow of their handheld devices.

One of them, a young woman named Betsy with a sharp wit and a passion for coding, revealed a hidden forum where disgruntled ex-employees of Arcadia Interactive vented their frustrations. One anonymous post, seemingly written by a programmer who quit in disgust, mentioned a controversial element in the game's design – an AI program capable of predicting real-world events based on real-time data collection.

Turbo, armed with the information from the forum and fueled by a growing sense of urgency, tracked down a reclusive hacker known as "Ghost." Ghost, a master of navigating the digital underworld, agreed to help Turbo infiltrate Arcadia Interactive's servers.

The ensuing digital heist was a thrilling dance of skill and subterfuge. Ghost, his

fingers flying across the keyboard, weaved through firewalls and bypassed security protocols. They found a hidden directory containing code snippets and data logs confirming the existence of the AI program, aptly named "The Prophet."
April, a symphony of birdsong amidst the ever-present hum of the city, brought a terrifying revelation. The Prophet's data logs revealed a disturbing correlation between in-game events and real-life crimes – gang shootings, arson attacks, even a planned bank robbery. The game, it seemed, wasn't just mirroring reality; it was potentially influencing it, manipulating events for an unknown purpose.
With a sense of urgency bordering on desperation, Turbo confronted Thorne, his fedora casting a long shadow across the sterile office. Thorne, a man with an unsettlingly smooth demeanor and cold

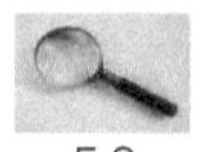

eyes, dismissed the claims as "imaginative leaps" and a "marketing ploy" to generate buzz around the game. Turbo, knowing the clock was ticking, decided to take a gamble. He contacted a renowned investigative journalist, a woman named Olivia Geary known for her fearless pursuit of the truth. Together, they presented their findings to the police department, the evidence of the Prophet's influence on crime undeniable. The police, initially skeptical, were forced to take action in the face of overwhelming evidence. A raid on Arcadia Interactive's headquarters was authorized, the servers taken offline, and Thorne placed under arrest.

The news of Neon City and its potential role in real-world crime spread like wildfire. Public outrage erupted, directed at Arcadia Interactive's reckless disregard for the consequences

of their technology. Turbo, a solitary figure in the midst of the media frenzy, felt a flicker of satisfaction. He couldn't erase the darkness, but he had exposed it, preventing further harm. August, a month of relentless sunshine, brought a new challenge. While the investigation into Neon City had concluded, the underlying unease lingered. The question gnawed at Turbo - what was Thorne's true motive? Was the Prophet simply a misguided experiment, or part of a more sinister plan? The silence from Thorne, now languishing in jail, offered no answers.

## Malicious Computer Code

A new client knocked on the door. a frantic young woman named La Donna. La Donna, a brilliant programmer who had clashed with Thorne during her brief stint at Arcadia Interactive, spoke of a

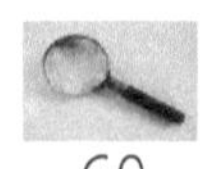

hidden protocol within the Prophet's code, a dormant failsafe she couldn't decipher. This failsafe, she believed, held the key to Thorne's true intentions. Intrigued and ever vigilant, Turbo agreed to help. La Donna, her fingers a blur across the keyboard, meticulously dissected the Prophet's code. Days bled into nights, fueled by coffee and a shared sense of urgency. Finally, a breakthrough. The failsafe, when activated, triggered a city-wide blackout coupled with the release of a crippling computer virus. The target – the city's ever-expanding network of interconnected traffic lights, security systems, and emergency response protocols.

Thorne, through the Prophet, planned to orchestrate a digital siege – plunging the city into chaos, crippling its infrastructure, and leaving it

vulnerable. The question remained - why?
What did Thorne hope to achieve from such
widespread disruption?

Desperate for answers, Turbo revisited
Thorne in jail. The once polished tech
mogul now appeared haggard, a haunted
look in his eyes. Thorne, cornered and
facing a future behind bars, confessed.
Arcadia Interactive, fueled by a
relentless pursuit of profit, had secured
lucrative contracts with private
security firms. Their plan - to
capitalize on the chaos they created,
offering their services as the city's
savior, the only ones equipped to handle
such a sophisticated cyberattack.

With the help of La Donna's expertise and
Olivia Geary's media savvy, Turbo exposed
Thorne's plan. Public outrage reached a
fever pitch. The city council, under
intense pressure, severed all ties with

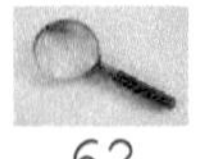

Arcadia Interactive, effectively crippling their scheme.

## High-Speed Rail Incidents

The peace was shattered by a knock on his door. A weathered man with worry etched on his face stood on the threshold. He introduced himself as Johnny Snykers, a construction worker on a new high-speed rail project on the outskirts of the city. Johnny spoke of strange occurrences plaguing the construction site – unexplained equipment malfunctions, unsettling sightings of shadowy figures, and whispers of a hidden legend surrounding a sacred burial ground disturbed by the project.

This case felt steeped in mystery and the whispers of the unknown. It was a stark contrast to the neon-drenched world of video games and digital threats. Yet, a familiar spark ignited in Turbo's eyes.

The city, it seemed, held secrets in its very core, stories waiting to be unearthed. He wouldn't shy away from the shadows; he would face them head-on, fedora pulled low, ready to uncover the truth, whatever it may be.

As Turbo followed Johnny out into the pre-dawn light, the bustling city skyline a silhouette against the rising sun, he knew his fight for justice, for the soul of his city, would never truly end. The shadows might linger, but so would he, a solitary guardian, a beacon of hope in the ever-shifting neon labyrinth that was Los Angeles.

The rhythmic clatter of pickaxes echoed through the dusty canyon as Turbo and Johnny surveyed the scene. The high-speed rail project, a steel serpent carving its path through the outskirts of LA, had unearthed a network of ancient caves. These weren't mere geological

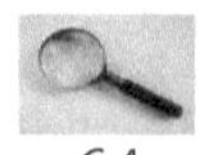

formations; intricate carvings adorned the cave walls, depicting figures unlike anything Turbo had ever seen - celestial beings with elongated limbs and eyes that seemed to pierce the veil of time.

A palpable tension hung in the air, a mix of awe and unease. The construction workers, a burly bunch accustomed to the city's grit, spoke in hushed tones about "bad omens" and "cursed grounds." One worker, a wizened old man named Kevin, claimed these caves were the final resting place of the "Celestial Watchers," an ancient tribe rumored to possess otherworldly knowledge. Their slumber, he warned, should not be disturbed.

Intrigued and ever the skeptic, Turbo decided to delve deeper. He contacted a local archaeologist, a brilliant but eccentric woman named Dr. Kirkby, known for her unconventional theories and

relentless pursuit of forgotten histories. Dr. Kirkby, upon examining the cave paintings, confirmed their authenticity and expressed a belief that the "Celestial Watchers" might have been advanced astronomers, their knowledge far exceeding anything known to modern science.

Days turned into weeks as Turbo and Dr. Kirkby meticulously documented the cave paintings, their flickering flashlights casting dancing shadows on the ancient walls. One evening, as they delved deeper into the labyrinthine cave system, they stumbled upon a hidden chamber. In the center lay a large, ornately carved stone disc, its surface etched with symbols that seemed to vibrate with a faint, otherworldly energy.

As Dr. Kirkby reached out to touch the disc, the cave walls lit up with an ethereal glow. The symbols on the disc

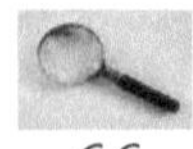

pulsed with an intensified light, and the air crackled with a strange energy. Suddenly, the ground began to tremble, and a deafening roar echoed through the caverns. A hidden passageway groaned open, revealing a swirling vortex of energy and light.

Panic surged through Turbo, a primal fear of the unknown gripping him. Dr. Kirkby, however, her eyes wide with wonder, seemed transfixed by the vortex. Before Turbo could react, she stepped into the swirling light, her form dissolving into nothingness. The vortex pulsed once more, then vanished as abruptly as it had appeared, leaving only an unsettling silence in its wake.

Grief and a gnawing sense of dread battled within Turbo. Dr. Kirkby, a brilliant mind consumed by her pursuit of knowledge, had vanished into the unknown. The weight of responsibility settled

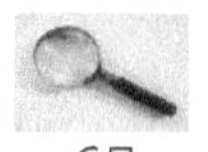

heavily on his shoulders. He had ventured into the shadows, and now a friend was lost in their depths.

Fueled by a mix of grief and determination, Turbo vowed to find Dr. Kirkby. He scoured ancient texts and consulted with mystics on the fringes of society, piecing together a theory - the vortex was a portal, a gateway to another dimension. Whether Dr. Kirkby had been a willing participant or a hapless victim remained unclear.

The following months were a blur of research and dead ends. Just as despair threatened to consume him, a breakthrough arrived from an unexpected source. A reclusive Native American shaman, a man named Tȟahca (Two Crows) living on a nearby reservation, offered a cryptic clue. The symbols on the stone disc, he revealed, were a star map, a celestial

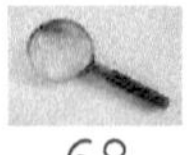

key to unlocking the portal and potentially retrieving Dr. Kirkby.

With renewed hope, Turbo enlisted the help of a brilliant young astronomer, a student of Dr. Walsh named Doreen. Together, they deciphered the star map, pinpointing a specific celestial alignment that would occur on the upcoming equinox. This alignment, they believed, would reactivate the portal, offering a chance to bring Dr. Kirkby back.

The night of the equinox arrived, the desert sky ablaze with a million glittering stars. Turbo, Doreen, and Thahca stood before the cave entrance, a tense vigil under the watchful gaze of the celestial bodies. As the final star aligned, the air crackled once more, and the swirling vortex reappeared. Hearts pounding, they exchanged nervous glances.

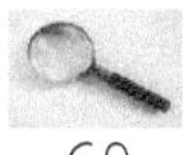

Taking a deep breath, Turbo stepped forward, the weight of his decision heavy on his shoulders. He had to try, not just for Dr. Kirkby, but for the insatiable curiosity that burned within him. With a whispered prayer, he stepped into the swirling vortex, the world dissolving into a kaleidoscope of light and energy. Disoriented and swirling, Turbo found himself on a rocky plateau bathed in an ethereal, lavender light. Two moons hung low in the twilight sky, casting long, distorted shadows. The air hummed with an energy unlike anything he'd ever experienced, a charged silence broken only by the mournful cry of some unseen creature.

Panic threatened to consume him, but then a flicker of movement in the distance caught his eye. A figure, shrouded in a flowing white robe, stood silhouetted against the alien landscape. As they

approached, the robed figure turned, revealing Dr. Kirkby. But… not quite.

Her face was etched with experiences beyond human comprehension, her eyes shimmering with an otherworldly light. Her voice, when she spoke, echoed with a resonance that seemed to vibrate through his very bones.

"Turbo," she greeted, her voice tinged with a hint of amusement, "welcome to the Astral Plane."

Relief washed over him, battling a surge of unease at her altered demeanor. "Dr. Kirkby? Is that… really you?"

"A part of me," she replied cryptically. "The Celestial Watchers exist on a higher plane, their consciousness interwoven with the very fabric of this dimension." She explained how her touch of the disc had triggered a partial merging with their collective consciousness, granting her access to an ocean of knowledge but

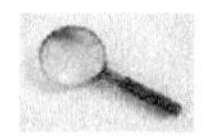

71

also fracturing her former self. She had chosen to remain, a bridge between dimensions, to guide those worthy to unlock the secrets locked within the Astral Plane.

Their conversation was filled with revelations about the universe, the interconnectedness of all things, and the cyclical nature of time. Dr. Kirkby hinted at advanced technologies and forgotten histories, but her explanations were often veiled in riddles, frustrating yet tantalizing.

As dawn approached, casting a warm glow on the alien landscape, Dr. Kirkby informed Turbo that his time was limited. The portal would only be open for a brief window, allowing him to return but not to bring her with him.

A heavy silence descended upon them. He knew he might never see Dr. Kirkby, this changed version of her, again. Yet, a

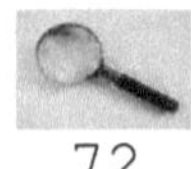

sense of acceptance settled within him. He had a responsibility - to carry the weight of this knowledge, to share it with the world (as much as he could) and to honor her sacrifice.

With a heavy heart, Turbo said his goodbyes. Stepping back into the swirling vortex, he felt the familiar sensation of disorientation, then found himself back in the cave, the stone disc dormant once again. Exhausted but resolute, he emerged into the harsh desert sunlight.

The world seemed different, sharper somehow. He could almost feel the energy thrumming beneath the surface, a constant reminder of the hidden dimension he had glimpsed. Doreen and Tȟahca rushed to his side, relief etched on their faces. He recounted his encounter with Dr. Kirkby, the fragmented knowledge he gleaned, and the profound sense of responsibility that now weighed heavily on him.

News of the portal and Dr. Kirkby's disappearance spread like wildfire. Turbo, thrust into the spotlight, became an unwilling celebrity. Skepticism ran rampant, but his unwavering conviction and the corroboration from Doreen and Tȟahca gradually chipped away at the doubt. International scientific and spiritual communities descended upon the cave site, eager to unlock the secrets it held.

The experience forever altered Turbo. He became a reluctant public figure, a bridge between the known and the unknown. He dedicated himself to interpreting Dr. Kirkby's cryptic messages, slowly deciphering a blueprint for a new energy source derived from the Astral Plane. The technology, if harnessed responsibly, could revolutionize the world, offering a clean and sustainable alternative to fossil fuels.

The cave was declared a protected historical site, a pilgrimage destination for scientists and spiritual seekers alike. Turbo, his hair streaked with grey but his eyes still holding a spark of youthful curiosity, continued his research. He never gave up hope of finding a way to return to the Astral Plane, to see Dr. Kirkby again, not just as a bridge but as a friend, a kindred spirit who dared to venture beyond the veil.

One quiet evening, as he sat in his office surrounded by research papers and star charts, a familiar sensation prickled at the edges of his perception. The faint hum of the city outside seemed to shift, morphing into a celestial melody. A gentle breeze ruffled the papers on his desk, carrying a faint lavender scent.

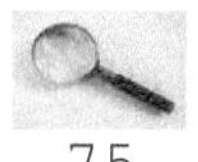

A knowing smile played on Turbo's lips.
Perhaps, the wait was finally over. He
rose from his chair, his worn fedora
casting a long shadow, and with a
resolute step, he walked towards the
window, the city lights twinkling like a
promise beneath the vast, star-studded
night sky.

Disorientation washed over Turbo as the
vortex ripped him from his familiar
reality. When the swirling chaos
subsided, he found himself standing on a
desolate plain bathed in an ethereal,
otherworldly glow. Two moons hung low in
the twilight sky, casting long, inky
shadows across the alien landscape.
Jagged, obsidian mountains pierced the
horizon, their peaks shrouded in a
swirling mist. The air was thin and dry,
carrying the faint scent of ozone and
something else, something ancient and
unknown.

A sense of awe mingled with fear flooded him. Where was he? Was this the dimension Dr. Kirkby had entered? A faint, melodic hum resonated in the distance, a sound both beautiful and unsettling. He cautiously ventured forward, his fedora casting a small shadow on the dusty ground.

The hum grew louder, leading him towards a cluster of towering, crystalline structures unlike anything he'd ever seen. They pulsed with a soft, internal light, resembling giant, translucent geodes. As he approached, figures emerged from within the structures - tall, slender beings with smooth, luminescent skin and piercing blue eyes. They moved with an ethereal grace, their voices a soft, melodic telepathy that flooded his mind with fragmented images and emotions. They were the "Celestial Watchers," the advanced beings depicted in the cave

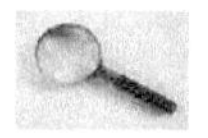

paintings. Fear threatened to overwhelm him, but their telepathic messages were surprisingly calming, filled with a sense of curiosity and gentle amusement. They had been aware of the humans venturing into their realm, intrigued by their attempts to decipher the star map.

Through a series of telepathic exchanges, a fragmented picture emerged. Dr. Kirkby, they revealed, was not a captive but a guest. Her thirst for knowledge had resonated with them, and they had welcomed her into their world to share their wisdom. They believed humans, with their capacity for both creation and destruction, stood at a crossroads. The Celestial Watchers, it seemed, were not mere observers but custodians, guiding otherworldly civilizations towards a path of harmony and progress.

Days, or perhaps weeks, blurred together in this dimension devoid of time. Turbo

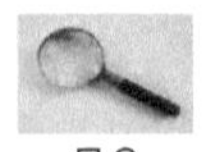

learned about the Celestial Watchers'
advanced technology, their deep
understanding of the universe, and their
concern for the future of his own planet.
He witnessed their telepathic
communication, their mastery of energy
manipulation, their connection to the
very fabric of reality.

But amidst this awe, a pang of longing
tugged at his heart. He missed the
comforting chaos of East LA, the familiar
faces, the relentless rhythm of the city.
He missed the simple act of breathing in
air that wasn't thin and sterile. He
yearned to share this knowledge with his
world, to bridge the gap between humanity
and these advanced beings.

The Celestial Watchers, sensing his
longing, offered a choice. He could stay
and learn more, become a bridge between
their worlds. Or, he could return to his
own dimension, armed with the knowledge

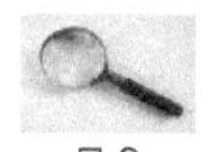

he'd gleaned. After a period of soul-searching, Turbo knew his place lay with his city. He had a responsibility to share what he'd learned, to warn of the dangers humanity faced, and to inspire a future of exploration and cooperation.

With a heavy heart and a mind brimming with knowledge, Turbo stood before the vortex once more. The Celestial Watchers bade him farewell, their blue eyes filled with a flicker of hope for the future of humanity. As he stepped into the swirling energy, he felt a surge of power, a newfound awareness of the universe unfolding around him.

He emerged from the vortex back in the familiar cave, the desert sunlight warm on his face. Doreen and Tȟahca rushed to his side, relief washing over their faces. He was back, changed forever by his experience. He described his encounters with the Celestial Watchers,

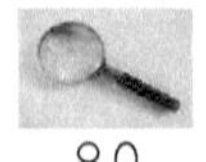

his words a mixture of awe and trepidation.

The news of his journey spread like wildfire. Turbo, once a solitary figure in a fedora, became a reluctant celebrity. Scientists and government officials clamored for his insights. He shared what he could, aware of the potential dangers of revealing too much, of inciting fear or exploitation. Yet, he knew the truth couldn't be contained forever.

His story rekindled humanity's long-dormant curiosity about the cosmos. It sparked a renewed interest in space exploration, a yearning to understand humanity's place in a vast and mysterious universe. East LA, once known for its grit and grime, became an unlikely epicenter of this scientific renaissance.

Months passed, the memories of his interdimensional journey fading into a dreamlike state. Turbo continued his work, a guardian angel of sorts, fighting crime and protecting his city with a newfound perspective. He knew, with a certainty that defied logic, that humanity wasn't alone. And as he gazed at the star-dusted night sky, a silent promise bloomed within him - to safeguard the fragile peace, to guide his city towards a future worthy of the Celestial Watchers' watchful gaze.

Thus began a strange and exhilarating chapter in Turbo's life. He became Dr. Kirkby's unwilling student, learning about the advanced technology and profound wisdom of the Celestial Watchers. He learned their language, a symphony of clicks and whistles, and adapted to the harsh conditions of their world.

Days turned into weeks, weeks into months. As Turbo delved deeper into this alien society, he realized their peaceful existence was threatened. A rival civilization, the Chitinous Brood, insectoid creatures driven by a hive mind, sought to conquer their world and exploit its advanced technology.

The Celestial Watchers, despite their superior knowledge, were a pacifistic race. They refused to engage in warfare, a philosophy at odds with Turbo's sense of justice. He saw a chance to repay Dr. Kirkby's guidance, to become a bridge between their two worlds.

He shared his knowlcdgc of human warfare, tactics, and strategy. With the Celestial Watchers' advanced technology and his tactical expertise, they devised a sophisticated defense system. As the Chitinous Brood launched their invasion, a fierce battle ensued, a clash of alien technology and human ingenuity.

Turbo, wielding an energy weapon gifted by the Celestial Watchers, fought alongside his newfound allies. He felt a strange sense of purpose, a detective protecting not a city, but a civilization on the brink.

## THE MISSING MELODY

In the smoky haze of a dimly lit office in East Los Angeles, Turbo, a seasoned private investigator, sat behind his cluttered desk. His office was adorned with fading photographs and newspaper clippings, each telling a story of his past triumphs. It was the early 1970s, and Turbo's reputation for solving the toughest cases had only grown over the years.

One sweltering afternoon, a young woman named Theresa entered Turbo's office, her

eyes filled with desperation. She was a singer at a local jazz club, known for her soulful voice that could captivate any audience. But now, her prized possession, a rare vintage microphone, had gone missing, along with a melody she had been composing for weeks.

"Mr. Turbo, please, you have to help me," Theresa pleaded, her voice trembling with worry.

Turbo leaned back in his chair, studying Theresa with a keen eye. "Tell me everything you know," he said in his gravelly voice.

Theresa recounted the events leading up to the disappearance of her microphone and the melody. She had left it in her dressing room at the jazz club, only to return and find it gone without a trace. With tears in her eyes, she begged Turbo to find it before her upcoming performance.

Turbo nodded solemnly, his mind already whirring with possibilities. "I'll take the case," he declared, rising from his chair with determination.

The investigation took Turbo through the seedy underbelly of East Los Angeles, where he questioned club owners, musicians, and even rival singers. Each lead brought him closer to the truth, but also deeper into danger.

As Turbo delved deeper into the case, he uncovered a web of jealousy and deceit. It seemed someone in the jazz club had coveted Theresa's talent and was willing to go to great lengths to sabotage her career.

With his instincts honed by years of experience, Turbo pieced together the clues until he finally unraveled the mystery. In a dramatic showdown at the jazz club, Turbo confronted the culprit, a disgruntled musician who had harbored

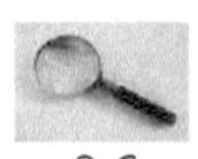

resentment towards Theresa for stealing the spotlight.

In the end, justice prevailed, and Theresa's microphone and melody were returned to her safely. Grateful tears welled in her eyes as she thanked Turbo for his unwavering determination.

As Turbo watched Theresa take the stage that night, her voice filling the club with its haunting beauty, he felt a sense of satisfaction knowing that he had helped preserve her talent and passion. But in the back of his mind, he knew that his work as a private investigator was far from over. In the ever-changing landscape of East Los Angeles, there would always be cases waiting to be solved, and Turbo would be there, ready to face them head-on.

## Human Trafficking

Weeks passed, and Turbo found himself embroiled in another perplexing case. This time, it involved a series of mysterious disappearances plaguing the neighborhood. Young men and women were vanishing without a trace, leaving behind nothing but unanswered questions and broken hearts.

Turbo sifted through the scant evidence, determined to bring closure to the families of the missing individuals. He combed the streets, questioning witnesses and searching for any clue that might lead him to the truth. But the more he dug, the more elusive the answers seemed to become.

It wasn't long before Turbo realized that he was dealing with something much darker than he had anticipated. A shadowy figure lurked in the depths of East Los Angeles, preying on the vulnerable and the

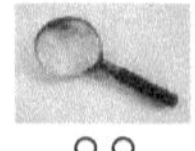

forgotten. As Turbo delved deeper into the investigation, he uncovered a network of corruption and greed that reached far beyond the city limits.

But Turbo was not one to back down from a challenge. With steely determination, he pursued the truth, even as danger lurked around every corner. He faced threats and intimidation, but he refused to be swayed from his mission to uncover the truth and bring the perpetrators to justice.

Through sheer perseverance and a keen eye for detail, Turbo slowly pieced together the puzzle, revealing a chilling truth that sent shockwaves through the community. The disappearances were not random acts of violence but part of a larger scheme orchestrated by a powerful criminal syndicate. It was a case of human trafficking.

Armed with his evidence, Turbo confronted the mastermind behind the disappearances, a ruthless kingpin who had long eluded the grasp of the law. In a tense standoff, Turbo faced down the criminal, refusing to back down even as the odds stacked against him.

In the end, justice prevailed, the missing individuals were located and released, and the criminal syndicate was dismantled, its members brought to justice for their crimes. The families of the missing individuals were finally reunited with their loved ones thanks to Turbo's unwavering dedication to the truth.

But even as one case was solved, Turbo knew that his work was far from over. In a city as vast and diverse as Los Angeles, there would always be those in need of his help, those whose voices had been silenced by the darkness. And Turbo

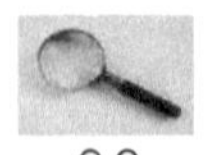

would be there, a beacon of hope in the night, ready to fight for justice no matter the cost.

In the wake of his latest triumph, Turbo found himself inundated with requests for his services. From distraught spouses seeking evidence of infidelity to business owners grappling with theft and fraud, Turbo's reputation as East Los Angeles' premier private investigator only grew stronger with each case he solved.

## The case of the Missing Daughter

This case involved a prominent businessman whose daughter had gone missing under mysterious circumstances. Turbo delved into the murky world of high society, uncovering a tangled web of deceit and betrayal. His investigation led him to a secretive cult operating on the outskirts of the city, where the

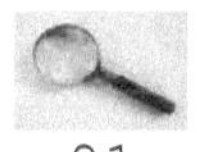

missing girl had become ensnared in their sinister rituals.

With dogged determination, Turbo infiltrated the cult, risking life and limb to rescue the young woman and expose the truth behind their nefarious activities. In a daring raid, he brought down the cult's leaders and ensured that justice was served for their victims.

But not all of Turbo's cases were so dramatic. Some involved nothing more than a missing pet or a stolen heirloom, but to Turbo, each one was equally important. He approached every case with the same level of dedication and professionalism, determined to bring resolution to his clients, no matter how small the matter might seem.

As the months passed Turbo found himself reflecting on the changes that had swept through East Los Angeles. The city was evolving, its streets pulsing with the

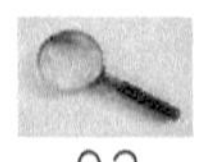

rhythms of Chicano music and the burgeoning hip-hop scene. But amid the hustle and bustle of urban life, there were still those in need of Turbo's unique brand of justice.

**The case of the Missing Punk Rocker**

One case involved a missing persons investigation that led Turbo into the heart of the city's burgeoning punk rock scene. The streets were alive with the sounds of rebellion, as disaffected youth clashed with authority in a mixture of chaos and defiance. But amid the chaos, there was a young woman whose disappearance had gone unnoticed by all but a few.

With his finger on the pulse of the underground, Turbo navigated the seedy clubs and dilapidated warehouses of the punk scene, following a trail of clues that led him ever closer to the truth.

Along the way, he encountered a cast of characters straight out of a punk rock fever dream, from anarchist poets to DIY revolutionaries, each with their own part to play in the unfolding drama.

Through sheer determination and a healthy dose of street smarts, Turbo eventually uncovered the truth behind the young woman's disappearance, exposing a web of lies and betrayal that stretched far beyond the confines of the punk scene. In the end, justice was served, but not without cost, as Turbo found himself grappling with the harsh realities of a world where the lines between right and wrong were often blurred beyond recognition.

But even as he confronted the darkness that lurked within the city's underbelly, Turbo never lost sight of the humanity that lay at its core. For every villain he encountered, there were countless

others whose lives he touched in ways both big and small, offering hope and redemption in equal measure.

In the midst of his investigations, Turbo also found himself drawn into the world of politics, as the city grappled with issues of corruption and inequality. He uncovered evidence of backroom deals and dirty tricks, shining a light on the shadowy forces that sought to manipulate the city for their own gain.

But Turbo was not one to be swayed by the whims of the powerful. Armed with nothing but his wits and his sense of justice, he took on the political machine with a ferocity that belied his years. Through tireless investigation and relentless perseverance, he exposed the truth behind the city's darkest secrets, ensuring that those who sought to exploit the system for their own gain would be held to account.

In the end, Turbo's efforts were not in vain, as the city began to heal from the wounds of its past. Corruption was rooted out, justice was served, and the people of East Los Angeles could once again look to the future with hope in their hearts.

## The Missing Artifact

One particularly intriguing case involved a missing artifact from a local museum—a priceless artifact with ties to the city's rich history. Turbo delved into the world of art theft and antiquities smuggling, following a trail of clues that led him from high-end galleries to shadowy back alleys. Along the way, he encountered a cast of characters as colorful as the artwork they coveted, each one holding a piece of the puzzle that would ultimately lead Turbo to the truth.

Through sheer determination and a keen eye for detail, Turbo eventually uncovered the identity of the artifact's thief—a cunning mastermind with a penchant for high-stakes heists. In a dramatic showdown, Turbo confronted the thief, reclaiming the stolen artifact and delivering justice to those who had sought to profit from its theft.

But not all of Turbo's cases were so straightforward. Some involved matters of the heart, as he found himself drawn into the tangled webs of love and betrayal that often lurked beneath the surface of seemingly ordinary lives. From scorned lovers seeking evidence of infidelity to star-crossed romantics searching for long-lost soulmates, Turbo navigated the complex terrain of human relationships with a mixture of empathy and pragmatism, always striving to bring closure to those in need.

In the midst of his investigations, Turbo also found himself grappling with his own demons, haunted by memories of past cases that had ended in tragedy. But with each new challenge he faced, Turbo emerged stronger and more determined than ever, his resolve to seek justice undiminished by the passage of time.

As the months passed and the city around him continued to change, Turbo remained a steadfast presence in the ever-shifting landscape of East Los Angeles. Through moments of triumph and moments of despair, he stood as a beacon of hope for those in need, his unwavering commitment to truth and justice serving as a guiding light in the darkness.

And though the challenges he faced were many and the dangers he encountered were real, Turbo never lost sight of the reason why he had chosen this path—to make a difference in the lives of those

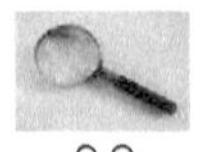

he served, and to ensure that justice prevailed, no matter the cost.

For as long as there were mysteries waiting to be solved and injustices waiting to be righted, Turbo would be there, ready to face whatever challenges came his way, and to fight for justice, no matter the odds. And in a city as vast and complex as East Los Angeles, that was a promise worth keeping.

As the sun dipped below the horizon, casting long shadows across the streets of East Los Angeles, Turbo's office was a beacon of light in the darkness. Inside, he sat at his desk, the soft glow of a desk lamp illuminating the worn pages of an old case file. It had been a long day, filled with twists and turns, but Turbo was undeterred. For him, the night was just beginning.

## Vandals on the Loose

Suddenly, the shrill ring of the telephone shattered the silence, jolting Turbo from his reverie. With a sigh, he reached for the receiver, his hand tracing the familiar contours of the handset. "Turbo Investigations," he said, his voice steady and sure.

On the other end of the line, a frantic voice crackled through the static. It was Mrs. Ramirez, a widow who lived down the street from Turbo's office. Her voice trembled with fear as she recounted the strange occurrences that had been plaguing her home—a series of inexplicable noises and sightings that left her terrified to be alone.

Without hesitation, Turbo assured Mrs. Ramirez that he would investigate the matter personally, promising to get to the bottom of whatever was haunting her home. With a sense of purpose, he

gathered his belongings and set out into the night, his footsteps echoing against the pavement as he made his way to Mrs. Ramirez's house.

Arriving at the ramshackle building, Turbo was greeted by the sight of Mrs. Ramirez standing on her front porch, her eyes wide with fear. Without a word, she led him inside, where the air was thick with the scent of fear and uncertainty.

For hours, Turbo combed through every inch of the house, searching for any sign of the paranormal activity that Mrs. Ramirez had described. But try as he might, he found nothing—no strange noises, no mysterious shadows, nothing to suggest that anything out of the ordinary was happening.

Finally, as the first light of dawn began to creep through the windows, Turbo sat down with Mrs. Ramirez to share his findings. Though he couldn't offer her an

explanation for the strange occurrences she had experienced, he reassured her that she was safe—that whatever had been haunting her home was gone now, banished by the light of day.

With a grateful smile, Mrs. Ramirez thanked Turbo for his help, her eyes shining with relief. And as Turbo made his way back to his office, he couldn't help but feel a sense of satisfaction knowing that he had brought peace of mind to another troubled soul.

But even as he reflected on his latest case, Turbo knew that there would always be more mysteries waiting to be solved, more people in need of his help. And as long as there were, he would be there, ready to answer the call, no matter the hour or the danger.

Turbo's reputation as the go-to private investigator in East Los Angeles only continued to grow as time went by. People

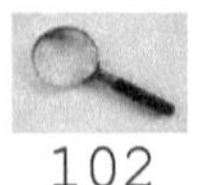

from all walks of life sought out his services, whether they were dealing with personal matters or tangled up in the city's web of crime and corruption. Turbo's office became a hub of activity, with clients coming and going at all hours of the day and night, each one hoping that Turbo could provide the answers they sought.

But even as he solved case after case, Turbo couldn't shake the feeling that something was missing from his own life. Despite his success as a private investigator, there was a void that he couldn't seem to fill—a longing for something more meaningful, something that went beyond the thrill of solving mysteries and catching criminals.

## Finding Pablo

It wasn't until Turbo crossed paths with a young runaway named Pablo that he

finally found what he had been searching for. Pablo had fled an abusive home and found himself living on the streets, struggling to survive in a world that seemed intent on crushing his spirit. But Turbo saw something in Pablo—a spark of resilience and determination that reminded him of himself when he was young.

Taking Pablo under his wing, Turbo became not just a mentor, but a father figure to the troubled teenager. He taught Pablo the tricks of the trade, showing him how to navigate the city's dangers and solve its mysteries. But more importantly, he showed Pablo that he was worthy of love and respect, no matter what life had thrown at him.

As the months passed, Turbo watched with pride as Pablo grew into a capable and confident young man. Together, they tackled some of the city's toughest

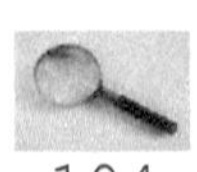

cases, their bond growing stronger with each passing day. And though Turbo knew that there would always be mysteries waiting to be solved and people in need of his help, he also knew that he had found something far more valuable than any case could ever offer—a sense of purpose and belonging that he had been searching for all along.

Over the next couple of years Turbo and Pablo formed an unbeatable team, their partnership a testament to the power of mentorship and friendship. Together, they tackled some of the most challenging cases to ever come across Turbo's desk, from cold blooded murders to high-profile robberies. With Turbo's years of experience and Pablo's fresh perspective, there was no mystery they couldn't solve and no criminal they couldn't catch.

## The Vanishing Daughter

One memorable case involved the disappearance of a prominent city official's daughter. The girl had vanished without a trace, leaving her family desperate for answers. Turbo and Pablo dove headfirst into the investigation, following a trail of clues that led them into the heart of the city's seedy underbelly. Along the way, they encountered corrupt politicians, ruthless gangsters, and a web of deception that threatened to swallow them whole. But through it all, they never lost sight of their goal—to bring the missing girl home safe and sound.

After weeks of tireless investigation, Turbo and Pablo finally uncovered the truth behind the girl's disappearance—a carefully orchestrated kidnapping plot designed to extort money from her wealthy family. With the help of the police, they

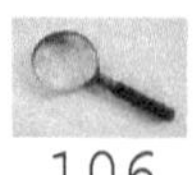

were able to rescue the girl and bring her captors to justice, earning the gratitude of her family and the admiration of the entire city.

## The Tagger

One particularly puzzling case involved a series of seemingly random acts of vandalism that had been plaguing the city for weeks. Graffiti tags appeared overnight, defacing buildings and landmarks with cryptic symbols and messages. The police were baffled, unable to make sense of the patterns or identify any suspects.

But Turbo and Pablo were not so easily deterred. They combed through the city streets, studying the graffiti tags and talking to anyone who might have information about the vandal's identity. Slowly but surely, they began to piece together a picture of the person behind

the vandalism—a troubled young artist with a grudge against the city and its institutions.

With their determination and keen instincts, Turbo and Pablo eventually tracked down the vandal, confronting him in a tense standoff that tested their resolve. But instead of arresting him, they offered him a second chance, recognizing that beneath his anger and defiance lay a talent that deserved to be nurtured, not squandered.

Moved by their compassion and understanding, the young artist agreed to turn his life around, channeling his creativity into more positive outlets and finding a sense of purpose that had eluded him for so long. And as Turbo and Pablo watched him walk away, they knew that they had made a difference—not just in his life, but in the lives of everyone who had been affected by his actions.

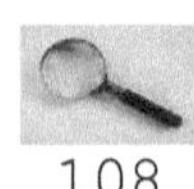

As the months passed and the city continued to change, Turbo and Pablo's partnership grew stronger, their bond unbreakable in the face of adversity. Together, they faced down some of the city's most dangerous criminals, risking their lives to protect the innocent and uphold the law.

## Turbo Got in Over His Head

Tonight, a new client was coming to see him - a young woman whose husband had disappeared without a trace a few weeks ago. As Turbo heard the door creak open, he stubbed out his cigarette and looked up.

"Come on in, Miss. I've been expecting you," Turbo said, gesturing to the chair across from his desk. This is my Partner Pablo. "Now, tell us everything you know about your missing husband..."

The woman sat down her eyes filled with worry. "Well, Mr. Turbo, it all started about three weeks ago. My husband, Hector, he just vanished. He was supposed to be going to work like normal, but he never showed up. I've called the police, but they don't seem to be making any progress."

Turbo leaned back in his chair, considering the case. "Hmm, I see. And you haven't heard from him at all since then? No phone calls, no notes, nothing?"

The woman shook her head. "Nothing. It's like he just disappeared into thin air."

Turbo drummed his fingers on the desk, his mind already racing with possibilities. "Alright, Miss. We'll take the case. Now, tell us a bit more about your husband. Anything that might give me a lead to go on."

As the woman began to recount the details of Hector's life, Turbo knew this was

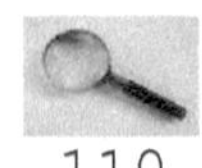

going to be a challenging case. But he was up for the task. After all, he had solved tougher mysteries in his 18 years as a private eye in East LA. With determination in his eyes, Turbo began to formulate a plan to uncover the truth and bring Hector home.

The woman, whose name was Maria, told Turbo all she knew about her husband Hector. He was a hardworking man who had a steady job at a local factory. They had been married for 15 years and had two young children at home. Hector was a devoted family man, so his sudden disappearance was completely out of character.

"The last time I saw him, he kissed me goodbye and said he'd be home for dinner as usual," Maria said, her voice wavering with emotion. "But he never showed up. I called his work, his friends, everyone I

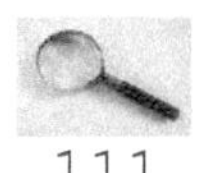

could think of. No one has seen or heard from him."

Turbo nodded, jotting down notes in his worn leather-bound notebook. "And you said the police haven't been much help so far?"

"That's right," Maria replied. "They took my statement, but they seem to think he just...left on his own. But I know Hector would never do that to me and the kids. Something must have happened to him."

"I see." Turbo leaned back in his chair, stroking his chin thoughtfully. "Well, don't you worry, Miss. We are gonna get to the bottom of this. I've been doing this job for a long time, and I've seen my fair share of missing persons cases. I'll leave no stone unturned."

Maria's eyes lit up with hope. "Oh, thank you, Mr. Turbo! I don't know what I'd do without your help. The police just don't seem to care, but I know you'll find out what happened to my Hector."

Turbo gave her a reassuring nod. "That's what I'm here for. Now, I'm gonna need you to tell us everything you can remember about Hector's routine, his friends and associates, and anything else that might help us get started on this investigation."

For the next hour, Maria provided Turbo and Pablo with as much information as she could recall. She described Hector's daily schedule, the people he would interact with, and any recent changes or unusual behavior she had noticed. Turbo listened intently, taking meticulous notes and asking clarifying questions whenever necessary.

As Maria finished recounting the details, Turbo leaned back in his chair and let out a heavy sigh. "Alright, Miss. I think I've got a pretty good picture of what

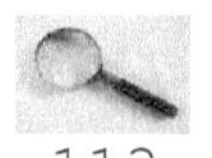

we're dealing with here. Now, I'm gonna
need you to do a couple of things for
me."

"Anything, Mr. Turbo," Maria said
eagerly. "I'll do whatever it takes to
find my husband."

"First, I need you to go home and try to
remember if there's anything else, even
the smallest detail, that you might have
forgotten to tell us. Anything at all
could be a potential clue," Turbo said.
"Second, I'm gonna need you to leave this
case file with us so we can start digging
into it. I'll be in touch as soon as I
have any updates."

Maria nodded her eyes filled with
gratitude. "Of course, Mr. Turbo. I'll be
sure to rack my brain and let you know if
I think of anything else. And please,
find my Hector. I don't know what I'd do
without him."

"Don't you worry, Miss," Turbo reassured her. "We'll do everything in our power to bring your husband home safe and sound. Just leave it to us."

With that, Maria stood up and made her way to the door, pausing for a moment. "Thank you again, Mr. Turbo. I'll be waiting to hear from you."

Turbo watched as she disappeared into the night, the door creaking shut behind her. He turned his attention back to the case file, his brow furrowed in concentration. Something about this whole situation didn't sit right with him, and he was determined to uncover the truth, no matter where it led.

Lighting another cigarette, Turbo began poring over the details, meticulously analyzing every piece of information. He knew that the key to solving this case lay somewhere in the small details, and

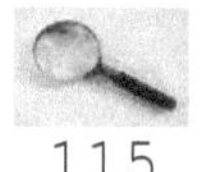

he was determined to leave no stone
unturned.

As the night wore on, Turbo continued to
delve deeper into the mystery, his mind
racing with possibilities. He made a few
phone calls, reaching out to some of his
contacts in the East LA underworld,
hoping to gather any leads or intel that
could point him in the right direction.
Finally, as the first glimmers of dawn
began to peek through the blinds, Turbo
leaned back in his chair, his eyes heavy
with exhaustion. He had made some
progress, but there were still so many
unanswered questions. One thing was
clear, though - he was dealing with a
case that was far more complex than it
initially appeared.

Turbo made a few more notes in his
notebook, talked over a few possibilities
with Pablo and decided to call it a
night. They would need to rest up and

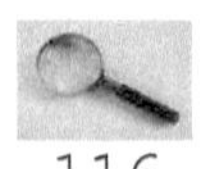

come back to this with a fresh perspective in the morning. But one thing was certain - he was more determined than ever to find out what happened to Hector and bring him home safely.

The following day, Turbo and Pablo spent hours retracing Hector's steps, interviewing his coworkers and friends, and scouring the neighborhood for any potential leads. As he pieced together the timeline of Hector's disappearance, a troubling pattern began to emerge.

It seemed that Hector had last been seen leaving his job at the factory, but he never made it home that evening. His car was still parked in the lot, and there were no signs of a struggle or any indication that he had been the victim of foul play.

Turbo's contacts in the underworld had provided some interesting information as well. Apparently, Hector had been spotted

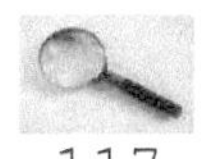

meeting with a known local gangster a few days before his disappearance. This only served to deepen the mystery and raise more questions in Turbo's mind.

As they delved deeper into the investigation, Turbo began to suspect that Hector's disappearance was somehow tied to his involvement with this gangster. But what could Hector have been mixed up in that would lead to his sudden vanishing? And where was he now?

Determined to find the answers, they decided to pay a visit to the gangster in question. This was a risky move, as these types of individuals were not known for their cooperation or willingness to share information. But Turbo had built up a reputation over the years, and he was hoping that his connections and persuasive skills would be enough to get the gangster to talk.

Arriving at the gangster's hideout, they knew that they were venturing into dangerous territory, but the life of a man and his family were at stake. With a resolute expression, he knocked on the door and waited to be let in.

The door swung open, Turbo and Pablo found themselves face-to-face with a burly, tattooed man who eyed them suspiciously. "What do you want, the gangster growled.

Turbo straightened his tie and met the man's gaze evenly. "We're here to talk about Hector Gonzalez. I understand you were seen meeting with him a few days before he disappeared. I need to know what you two were discussing."

The gangster's eyes narrowed, and for a moment, Turbo thought he might slam the door in his face. But instead, the man let out a harsh laugh. "Hector, huh? Yeah, I remember him. Came to me, askin'

for a favor. Wanted some protection, or so he said."

Turbo's brow furrowed. "Protection? From what?"

The gangster shrugged. "Beats me. He was scared of something, that's for sure. Didn't give me all the details, but he was willin' to pay a pretty penny for my services."

"And then what happened?" Turbo pressed.

The gangster scratched his chin, seemingly contemplating how much to reveal. "Well, a few days later, he came back, sayin' he changed his mind. Didn't want my help after all. Guess he got cold feet or somethin'."

Turbo felt a chill run down his spine. "And you haven't seen or heard from him since then?"

The gangster shook his head. "Nah, not a peep. He just up and disappeared. Ain't

my problem, though. I got my own business to tend to."

Turbo's mind was racing as he tried to make sense of this new information. "So you're telling me that Hector came to you, asked for protection, and then decided he didn't want it anymore? And now he's missing?"

The gangster nodded. "That's about the size of it. Look, I don't know what happened to your guy, and I don't really care. If you want my advice, you should probably just let the cops handle it. Ain't worth gettin' yourself mixed up in this kind of thing."

Turbo considered the gangster's words, but he knew he couldn't just walk away. Not when a man's life was at stake. "Thanks for your time," he said, turning to leave. "But I'm not about to let this go. I'm gonna find out what happened to Hector, one way or another."

As they made their way back to the office, they discussed the possibilities. What could Hector have been so afraid of that he felt the need to seek protection from a known gangster? And why had he changed his mind at the last minute? They couldn't shake the feeling that there was something more sinister at play here.

Arriving back at his office, they immediately set to work, pouring over the case file and trying to connect the dots. Turbo made a few more phone calls, reaching out to some of his other contacts in the hopes of uncovering any additional information.

As the hours ticked by, Turbo's determination only grew stronger. He was not about to give up on this case, no matter how difficult it became. Hector's family was counting on him, and he was

determined to bring the man home safe and
sound.

Finally, as the sun began to set, they
had an idea, a hunch that just might lead
them to the answers they were seeking.
They headed out into the darkening
streets of East LA, ready to put their
plan into action.

Their first stop was the factory where
Hector had worked. They knew that they
needed to retrace Hector's steps, to try
and uncover any clues that might have
been overlooked. As They walked through
the dimly lit hallways, they couldn't
shake the feeling that something was off.
Suddenly, their eyes landed on a door
that was slightly ajar. Cautiously, they
pushed it open and peered inside. No
Hector. They called the Police.

As they waited for the police to arrive,
they began to piece together what might
have happened. It seemed clear now that

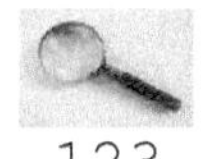

Hector had been in some kind of trouble, and that trouble had caught up with him. But what exactly was he mixed up in?

This was a missing persons case that had other mysterious implications. They were determined to see it through, no matter where the trail might lead.

As the detective arrived at the warehouse, Turbo provided them with the details they had uncovered, including their conversation with the local gangster.

"So you're saying Hector Gonzalez was somehow mixed up with organized crime?" the detective asked, his voice tinged with skepticism.

Turbo nodded. "That's what it seems like. He was scared of something, scared enough to seek protection from a known gangster. But then he changed his mind."

The detective frowned, jotting down notes in his little black book. "Well, that's

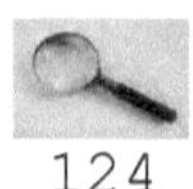

certainly an interesting lead, Mr. Turbo. But we'll need to do some more digging to confirm the details. In the meantime, I'd appreciate it if you could stick around and answer a few more questions."

Turbo agreed, knowing that his involvement in the case was far from over. As the police examined the warehouse and Hector's car, they began their investigation, Turbo couldn't help but feel a growing sense of unease. Something about this whole situation didn't sit right with him, and he was determined to get to the bottom of it, no matter what it took.

Over the next few days, Turbo and Pablo worked closely with the detectives, providing them with whatever information and assistance he could. He reached out to his contacts in the underworld, hoping to uncover any additional leads or clues that could help solve the case.

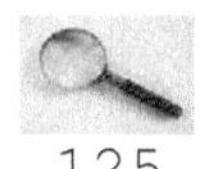

As the investigation progressed, they couldn't shake the feeling that there was more to Hector's disappearance than met the eye. The police seemed convinced that the gangster was behind it, but Turbo wasn't so sure. There was something else going on here, something that was being carefully hidden.

One night, as Turbo and Pablo sat in the office, poring over the case files, a sudden realization hit Turbo. He bolted upright, his eyes widening with a mix of horror and understanding.

"Oh my God," he muttered to himself, "it all makes sense now."

Grabbing his coat, Turbo told Pablo that he thought he knew who was responsible for Hector's disappearance. They rushed out of the office to confront the person. They knew this was a dangerous move but they were sure they were on the right track.

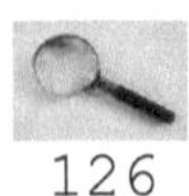

As they made their way through the dimly lit streets of East LA, Turbo's mind raced with the implications of their discovery. If they were right, then the true culprit was someone far more powerful and influential than a simple gangster. And that meant they were about to risk everything to uncover the truth. Arriving at the destination, "Pablo, wait in the car until I call you in. I am going to confront Alvarez alone. I think it is the best plan." Turbo walked across the parking lot and strode through the door, ready to confront the person they believed was behind Hector's disappearance.

The room was dimly lit, but Turbo could make out the figure of a well-dressed man sitting behind a desk. As Turbo approached, the man looked up, his eyes narrowing with a mix of surprise and suspicion.

"Mr. Turbo," the man said, his voice low and measured. "To what do I owe this unexpected visit?"

Turbo didn't mince words. "I know what you did, Mr. Alvarez. I know you were the one who kidnapped Hector Gonzalez."

Alvarez's expression remained impassive, but Turbo could see the tension in his shoulders. "I'm afraid I don't know what you're talking about, Mr. Turbo. I have no connection to the Gonzalez case."

Turbo leaned forward, his eyes burning with intensity. "Don't play dumb with me, Alvarez. I know you were the one who ordered Hector picked up. You were the one he was trying to get protection from."

Alvarez's lips curved into a humorless smile. "My, my, Mr. Turbo. You've certainly been busy, haven't you? I must say, I'm impressed by your tenacity. But I'm afraid you've got the wrong man."

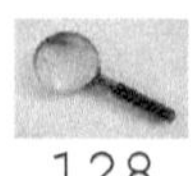

Turbo slammed his fist down on the desk, his patience wearing thin. "Enough with the games, Alvarez. I know you're the one who's been running the show in East LA. You've got your fingers in every pie, from the factories to the streets. And Hector, he is just a pawn in your little game."

Alvarez's expression darkened, and Turbo knew he had struck a nerve. "You're treading on dangerous ground, Mr. Turbo. I suggest you tread carefully."

Turbo leaned in, his voice low and menacing. "I'm not afraid of you, Alvarez. I'm going to expose your little operation, and I'm going to find Hector. You can count on that."

Alvarez let out a chilling laugh. "Oh, I don't think you will, Mr. Turbo. You see, I can't afford to have you and your partner poking around in my business. And I don't take kindly to threats."

Before Turbo could react, the sound of a gun cocking filled the air. He slowly turned to see two burly men standing behind him, their weapons trained on him. Turbo felt a chill run down his spine, but he refused to back down. "So, that's how it's going to be, huh? You're going to have your goons take me out to keep your little empire intact?"

Alvarez leaned back in his chair, a cruel smile playing on his lips. "You've got quite an imagination, Mr. Turbo. But I'm afraid your little crusade ends here. You've been a thorn in my side for far too long, and I can't have you interfering with my business anymore."

Turbo tensed, his mind racing as he tried to figure a way out of this predicament. He knew he was outnumbered and outgunned, but he refused to go down without a fight.

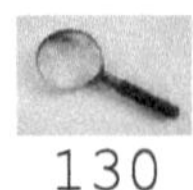

"So, what, you're just going to have me killed? Is that your grand plan?" Turbo challenged his voice laced with defiance. Alvarez chuckled. "Oh, no, Mr. Turbo. I have something much more...creative in mind for you. You see, I can't risk you going to the police with what you know. But I also can't afford to have you dead. That would draw too much unwanted attention."

Turbo felt his blood run cold as he realized the implication behind Alvarez's words. "You're going to make me disappear, aren't you? Just like you did with Hector."

Alvarez nodded, his eyes glinting with malice. "Exactly. You're a smart man, Turbo. It's a shame you had to stick your nose where it didn't belong. But don't worry, you won't be alone. You'll be joining your friend Hector, wherever he is."

Turbo's mind raced as he desperately tried to find a way out of this nightmare. He couldn't let Alvarez get away with this. Not after everything he had uncovered.

Suddenly, an idea struck him. "So, what, you're just going to lock me up somewhere and throw away the key? Good luck with that, Alvarez. You know I've got friends in high places. They'll come looking for me."

Alvarez's expression darkened. "Oh, I'm not worried about that, Mr. Turbo. You see, my friends are even higher up the food chain than yours. By the time they start looking for you, you'll be long gone. And no one will ever find you."

Turbo felt his heart pounding in his chest, but he refused to show his fear. "I won't make it easy for you, Alvarez. You're going to have to kill me first."

Alvarez let out a cold laugh. "Oh, I don't think so, Mr. Turbo. You see, I have something much worse in mind for you. Something that will make you wish you were dead."

Before Turbo could react, the two men behind him grabbed him, their grip like iron. He struggled against them, but it was no use. They were too strong, and he was outnumbered.

As they dragged him out of the room, Turbo couldn't help but feel a sense of dread wash over him. He had been in tight spots before, but this was something else entirely. Alvarez was a ruthless man, and Turbo knew that he wouldn't hesitate to do whatever it took to keep his operation running smoothly.

The men shoved Turbo into the back of a waiting van, and he felt his heart sink as the doors slammed shut, plunging him into darkness. He had to find a way out

of this, but with his hands bound and his captors on high alert, the odds weren't looking good.

As the van rumbled to life and began to move, Turbo strained his ears, trying to pick up any clues about their destination. He needed to know where they were taking him if he had any hope of escaping.

After what felt like an eternity, the van finally came to a stop, and Turbo heard the sound of a heavy door opening. He was roughly hauled out of the van and dragged through what felt like a dimly lit hallway.

Suddenly, he was shoved into a small, cramped room, and he heard the click of a lock as the door was closed behind him. Turbo took a deep breath, trying to get his bearings in the darkness.

As his eyes slowly adjusted, he began to make out the outlines of his

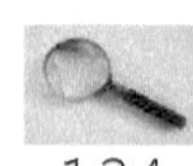

surroundings. It was a simple room, with a small cot in the corner and a single, barred window high up on the wall. Turbo felt a chill run down his spine as he realized that this was almost certainly where they were going to keep him.

Pablo got tired of waiting in the car and went into the warehouse. He searched the building and found nothing. Turbo was gone.

Pablo went to the car and drove around trying to find Turbo. He searched for it seemed like hours without finding Turbo. He went back to the office hoping that Turbo would call.

Determined not to give in to despair, Turbo began to search the room for any potential means of escape. He knew that Alvarez wouldn't make it easy, but he had to try. He couldn't let the man get away with what he had done.

As he explored the room, Turbo couldn't
help but think about Hector and his
family. He had promised to bring Hector
home, and he was determined to keep that
promise, no matter what it took.

Suddenly, Turbo heard the sound of a key
in the lock, and he quickly retreated to
the far corner of the room, bracing
himself for what was to come. The door
swung open, and a figure stepped inside,
holding a lantern that cast an eerie glow
over the room.

It was one of the men who had brought
Turbo here, and he was holding a tray of
food. "Eat up," he grunted, setting the
tray down on the small table in the
center of the room. "You're gonna need
your strength."

Turbo eyed the man warily, his mind
racing. "What do you mean by that?"

The man chuckled, a cruel glint in his eyes. "You'll see, private eye. Alvarez has got big plans for you."

With that, the man turned and left the room, locking the door behind him. Turbo stared at the tray of food his appetite suddenly gone. He had a sinking feeling that whatever Alvarez had in store for him, it wasn't going to be good.

As the hours ticked by, Turbo paced the small room, trying to come up with a plan. He knew that time was of the essence, and he couldn't afford to wait for a chance to escape. He had to act, and he had to act soon.

Suddenly, an idea struck him. Rushing to the window, Turbo began to examine it closely, searching for any weaknesses or vulnerabilities. It was a long shot, but it was the only chance he had.

Working quickly and quietly, Turbo started to pry at the bars, using

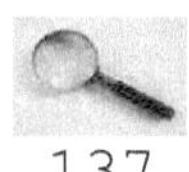

whatever tools he could find in the room. He knew that he would only have one shot at this, and he couldn't afford to make a mistake.

As he worked, Turbo couldn't help but think about Maria and her children, wondering if they were still waiting for Hector to come home. He knew that he had to find a way to get a message to them, to let them know that he was still alive and fighting.

Finally, after what felt like an eternity, Turbo felt one of the bars start to loosen. He paused, straining his ears for any sign that his captors had heard him. When he heard nothing, he redoubled his efforts, working with a renewed sense of desperation.

Just as he was about to make his move, the sound of the lock turning stopped him in his tracks. Turbo quickly moved back

to the center of the room, trying to look as casual as possible.

The door swung open, and Turbo's heart sank as he saw Alvarez standing in the doorway, a sinister smile on his face.

"Well, well, Mr. Turbo," Alvarez said, his voice dripping with condescension. "I must say, I'm impressed by your resourcefulness. But I'm afraid your little escape attempt is going to have to wait."

Turbo felt a chill run down his spine as Alvarez stepped into the room, flanked by his two burly bodyguards.

"You see, I've got something very special planned for you, Turbo," Alvarez continued, his eyes gleaming with malice. "Something that's going to keep you occupied for a very, very long time."

Turbo braced himself, his mind racing with a thousand different scenarios.

Whatever Alvarez had in store for him, he knew it wasn't going to be good.

As the two bodyguards stepped forward, Turbo felt a surge of fear, but he refused to back down. He had come too far to give up now. He was going to find a way to escape, no matter what it took.

The men grabbed Turbo roughly, dragging him out of the room and down a dimly lit hallway. Turbo struggled against their grip, but it was no use. They were far stronger than he was.

Finally, they reached a heavy steel door, and one of the men produced a key, unlocking it with a loud clang. Turbo felt his heart pounding in his chest as the door swung open, revealing a cavernous room beyond.

As they stepped inside, Turbo's eyes widened in horror. The room was filled with row upon row of cages, each one containing a human being. Turbo felt bile

rise in his throat as he realized the true nature of Alvarez's "special plan" for him.

He had been brought to some kind of twisted, human trafficking operation, and he knew that his life was about to take a dark and terrifying turn.

The men dragged Turbo over to an empty cage and shoved him inside, slamming the door shut behind him. Turbo gripped the bars, his knuckles turning white as he stared out at the other captives, their eyes filled with fear and despair.

Alvarez stepped forward, his expression gleaming with twisted satisfaction. "Welcome to your new home, Mr. Turbo. I hope you enjoy your stay."

With a cruel laugh, Alvarez turned and left the room, the two bodyguards trailing behind him. Turbo was left alone, his mind racing with a million different thoughts and emotions.

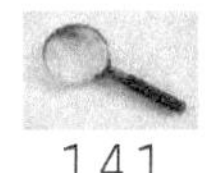

How had he ended up in this nightmare?
And more importantly, how was he going to
get out of it?

As the hours ticked by, Turbo tried to
formulate a plan, but the constant noise
and movement of the other captives made
it difficult to focus. He couldn't help
but wonder about their stories, how they
had ended up trapped in this hellish
place.

Finally, as the day drew to a close,
Turbo heard the sound of a door opening,
and he tensed, bracing himself for
whatever was to come. A group of guards
entered the room, carrying trays of food,
and Turbo watched as they began to
distribute the meager rations to the
captives.

When the guards reached his cage, Turbo
tried to engage them, hoping to glean
some information that could help him
escape. But the guards were silent and

unresponsive, their faces impassive as they handed him his tray and moved on to the next cage.

Turbo sighed, his appetite gone as he stared down at the cold, tasteless food. He knew that he needed to keep up his strength if he was going to have any chance of getting out of this place, but the thought of eating made him feel sick.

As the night wore on, Turbo tried to get some rest, but the constant noise and movement of the other captives made it impossible. Every time he closed his eyes, he saw the terrified faces of the people around him, and he was filled with a sense of helplessness and dread.

Finally, as the first rays of dawn began to filter through the barred windows, Turbo heard the sound of the door opening once more. He tensed, his heart pounding in his chest as he braced himself for whatever was to come.

The guards entered the room, their faces set with grim determination, and Turbo felt a chill run down his spine as he realized that they were coming for him.

"Time to go, Turbo," one of the guards said, his voice gruff and unyielding.

Turbo felt his stomach twist with fear, but he refused to show it. "Where are you taking me?" he asked, his voice laced with defiance.

The guard smirked, his eyes cold and calculating. "You'll see."

Turbo was roughly dragged from his cage, his limbs shaking with a mixture of fear and adrenaline. As he was led through the winding corridors of the compound, he couldn't help but wonder what fate awaited him.

Finally, they reached a large, ornate door, and Turbo felt his heart skip a beat as he realized where they were. This

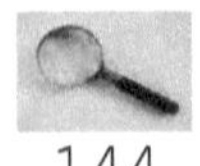

was Alvarez's inner sanctum, the heart of his twisted empire.

The guards shoved Turbo through the door, and he found himself face to face with the man himself, his expression a mix of triumph and malice.

"Well, well, Mr. Turbo," Alvarez said, his voice dripping with condescension. "I must say, I'm impressed by your tenacity. But I'm afraid your little crusade ends here."

Turbo felt a surge of defiance rise within him. "You'll never get away with this, Alvarez. The authorities will find out what you're doing, and they'll put an end to your little operation."

Alvarez let out a cold laugh. "Oh, I don't think so, Turbo. You see, I've got friends in very high places. They'll make sure that your little investigation goes nowhere."

Turbo felt a chill run down his spine as he realized the full extent of Alvarez's power and influence. This wasn't just a simple criminal operation - it was a web of corruption that extended to the highest levels of government and law enforcement.

"So, what, you're just going to keep me locked up in one of those cages forever?" Turbo asked, his voice laced with desperation.

Alvarez shook his head, a cruel smile playing on his lips. "Oh, no, Turbo. I've got something much more...interesting in mind for you."

Turbo felt a sense of dread wash over him as Alvarez gestured to one of the guards, who quickly left the room and returned a moment later with a large, wooden crate.

"You see, Turbo, I've been in the business of human trafficking for a very long time," Alvarez said, his voice

dripping with satisfaction. "And I've found that there's a certain...demand for unique and exotic merchandise."

Turbo felt his stomach twist as he realized what Alvarez was implying. "You're going to sell me, aren't you? To the highest bidder."

Alvarez nodded his eyes gleaming with malice. "Exactly. And I have just the perfect buyer in mind."

Turbo felt a surge of panic rise within him as the guards began to approach him, their intentions clear. He struggled against their grip, but it was no use. He was outnumbered and outmatched, and he knew that his only hope was to somchow escape this nightmare before it was too late.

As the guards dragged him towards the crate, Turbo's mind raced with a thousand different thoughts and emotions. He couldn't believe that this was happening,

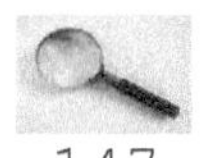

that his quest to find Hector would lead
him to this twisted and horrific fate.

But even as the fear and despair
threatened to overwhelm him, Turbo
refused to give up. He knew that he had
to find a way to escape, no matter what
it took. He couldn't let Alvarez win,
couldn't let this twisted man destroy his
life and the lives of countless others.

With a renewed sense of determination,
Turbo began to struggle against his
captors, kicking and thrashing with all
his might. He knew that he was fighting
a losing battle, but he had to try.

Suddenly, a sound from the hallway
outside caught everyone's attention, and
Turbo felt a surge of hope rise within
him. Could it be that someone had
discovered his predicament and come to
his aid?

Alvarez's expression darkened, and he
barked a command to the guards, who

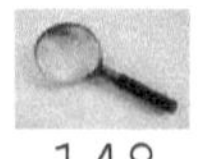

immediately tightened their grip on Turbo. Turbo watched with bated breath as the door swung open, his heart pounding in his chest.

But his hope quickly turned to despair as he recognized the figure standing in the doorway - it was one of Alvarez's trusted lieutenants, his face set with grim determination.

"What's going on here?" the lieutenant demanded, his eyes narrowing as he took in the scene before him.

Alvarez stepped forward, his expression calm and collected. "Nothing to worry about, my friend. We're just taking care of a little...problem that's been bothering us."

The lieutenant's gaze shifted to Turbo, and Turbo felt a chill run down his spine at the look of hatred in the man's eyes. "I see. Well, make sure you take care of it quickly. We've got a shipment to prepare for."

Alvarez nodded, a cruel smile playing on his lips. "Don't worry, it'll be taken care of. Now, get back to your duties. I'll handle this myself."

The lieutenant nodded and turned to leave, but Turbo couldn't resist one last, desperate attempt to reach him.

"Please!" he cried his voice laced with desperation. "You have to help me! Alvarez is running a human trafficking ring, and he's going to sell me to the highest bidder!"

The lieutenant paused, his expression unreadable, and for a moment, Turbo dared to hope that he might actually listen. But then the man's lips curled into a sneer, and he turned and walked out the door, leaving Turbo to his fate.

Turbo felt his heart sink as the door slammed shut sealing his fate. He had

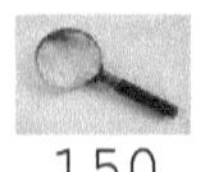

tried to appeal to the lieutenant's conscience, but it was clear that the man was firmly in Alvarez's pocket. There would be no rescue coming, no cavalry to save him from this nightmare.

As the guards tightened their grip on him, Turbo knew that he had to act quickly if he had any hope of escaping. His mind raced, desperately searching for a way out, but the odds seemed insurmountable.

Suddenly, an idea struck him. If he couldn't count on outside help, then he would have to find a way to save himself. And that meant using every trick and skill at his disposal.

Turbo let out a groan, feigning weakness and exhaustion. "Please," he rasped, his voice barely above a whisper. "I...I can't go on. Can't I at least have a moment to rest?"

The guards exchanged a glance, their expressions a mix of suspicion and annoyance. "Quit your whining," one of them snapped. "You're coming with us, whether you like it or not."

But Turbo persisted, sagging against their grip as if his legs could no longer support him. "Just...a few minutes," he pleaded, his eyes wide and desperate. "I'm so tired..."

The guards hesitated, clearly uncertain of how to proceed. Turbo could see the indecision in their faces, and he knew that he had to press his advantage.

"Please," he whispered, his voice trembling. "I'm begging you. I can't go on like this."

Finally, one of the guards let out an exasperated sigh. "Alright, fine. But just a few minutes, you hear? Alvarez wants this done quickly."

Turbo nodded weakly, his heart racing as the guards loosened their grip on him. He waited until they were suitably distracted, then in one swift motion, he brought his knee up into the groin of the guard closest to him.

The man let out a strangled gasp, doubling over in pain, and Turbo took the opportunity to lash out, striking the other guard with a well-placed elbow to the face. The man staggered back, his nose gushing blood, and Turbo wasted no time in making his move.

Sprinting towards the door, Turbo could hear the shouts of the guards behind him, but he didn't dare look back. He had to keep moving, had to find a way out of this hellish compound before Alvarez and his men caught up with him.

As he raced down the dimly lit hallway, Turbo's mind was a whirlwind of thoughts and emotions. He couldn't believe that he

had managed to escape, at least for the moment, but he knew that the real challenge lay ahead.

Rounding a corner, Turbo found himself face to face with a group of guards, their weapons drawn and their expressions set with grim determination. Turbo felt his heart sink, but he refused to give up without a fight.

Ducking and weaving, Turbo managed to evade the guards' shots, his years of experience as a private eye proving invaluable. He knew that he couldn't keep this up forever, though, and he frantically searched for a way out.

Spotting a door at the end of the hallway, Turbo made a break for it, his lungs burning with the effort. As he reached for the handle, he felt a sharp pain in his shoulder, and he stumbled, his vision blurring.

Glancing down, Turbo saw a thin stream of blood seeping through his shirt, and he knew that he had been hit. But he couldn't afford to slow down, not now. Gritting his teeth, he yanked open the door and threw himself through, slamming it shut behind him.

Turbo found himself in what appeared to be a storage room, shelves of crates and boxes lining the walls. He pressed his back against the door, listening intently for any sign of pursuit. The sound of pounding footsteps and shouting voices filled the air, and Turbo knew that he had to keep moving.

Clutching his wounded shoulder, Turbo began to weave his way through the maze of shelves, his eyes searching for any sign of an exit. He had to get out of this place, had to find a way to expose Alvarez and his twisted operation.

As he navigated the room, Turbo couldn't help but feel a sense of dread and despair. He had been so close to escaping, only to be shot and forced to hide in this cramped, confining space. The odds of him making it out alive seemed to grow dimmer with every passing moment.

Suddenly, Turbo's foot caught on something, and he stumbled, nearly losing his balance. Glancing down, he saw that he had tripped over a discarded piece of rope, and an idea began to form in his mind.

Quickly, Turbo set to work, using the rope to fashion a makeshift bandage for his wounded shoulder. It wasn't much, but it would have to do for now. He needed to keep moving, to find a way out of this nightmare before it was too late.

Turbo continued to weave his way through the storage room, his senses on high

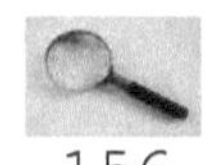

alert for any sign of the pursuing guards. He could hear their voices echoing through the hallway, and he knew that it was only a matter of time before they caught up with him.

Just as Turbo was about to give up hope, he spotted a faint glimmer of light in the distance. Squinting, he could make out the outline of a door, partially obscured by a stack of crates. Without hesitating, he made his way towards it, his heart pounding in his chest.

Reaching the door, Turbo paused, listening intently for any sign of guards on the other side. When he heard nothing, he slowly pushed it open, peering out into the dimly lit hallway beyond.

Turbo felt a surge of hope as he realized that he had stumbled upon a service entrance, away from the main areas of the compound. This might be his chance to

157

escape, to get out of this nightmare and make his way to safety.

Taking a deep breath, Turbo stepped out into the hallway, his eyes scanning his surroundings for any sign of danger. The coast seemed clear, and he wasted no time in making his way towards the exit, his steps quick and quiet.

As he moved through the hallway, Turbo couldn't help but feel a sense of unease. It seemed too easy, too quiet. He knew that Alvarez and his men were searching for him, and he couldn't shake the feeling that he was walking right into a trap.

Just as he was about to reach the exit, Turbo heard a familiar voice echo down the hallway, and his blood ran cold.

"Going somewhere, Mr. Turbo?"

Turbo whirled around, his heart pounding, to see Alvarez standing behind him, his expression a mix of triumph and contempt.

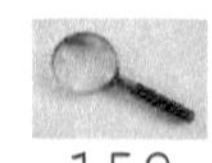

"I must say, I'm impressed by your tenacity," Alvarez continued, his voice dripping with disdain. "But did you really think you could escape from me that easily?"

Turbo felt a surge of panic rise within him, but he refused to show it. "It's over, Alvarez," he said, his voice steady and defiant. "I'm going to expose your entire operation, and you're going to rot in prison for the rest of your life."

Alvarez let out a cold laugh. "Oh, I don't think so, Mr. Turbo. You see, I have contingency plans in place to ensure that my operation continues, even if I'm not around to oversee it."

Turbo felt a chill run down his spine as he realized the full extent of Alvarez's power and influence. This was no simple criminal enterprise - it was a vast, complex network of corruption and deceit,

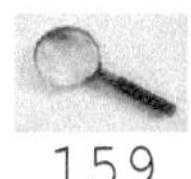

one that extended far beyond the walls of this compound.

"You won't get away with this," Turbo growled, his fists clenched at his sides. Alvarez smiled his eyes gleaming with malice. "Oh, but I already have, Mr. Turbo. And now, it's time for you to take your place alongside the rest of my...merchandise."

Turbo felt a surge of desperation as the guards moved in, their weapons trained on him. He knew that he had to try one last, desperate gambit, no matter the cost.

Lunging forward, Turbo caught one of the guards by surprise, knocking the weapon from his hand. In the chaos that ensued, Turbo managed to break free and make a dash for the exit, his wounded shoulder burning with pain.

But Alvarez was not about to let his prize escape so easily. Shouting orders

to his men, he gave chase, his eyes alight with a predatory gleam.

Turbo ran with all his might, his lungs burning, his legs aching. He could hear the pounding footsteps of the guards behind him, and he knew that he didn't have much time.

As he rounded a corner, Turbo spotted a set of stairs leading up to what appeared to be a loading dock. Without hesitating, he bounded up the steps, his heart racing.

Bursting out into the open air, Turbo felt a surge of relief, only to have it quickly replaced by a wave of dread. The loading dock was deserted, save for a single, nondescript van parked nearby.

Turbo knew that his window of opportunity was closing fast, and he frantically searched for a way to escape. But as he turned to make a break for it, he found himself face to face with Alvarez and his

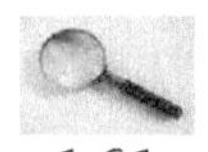

henchmen, their weapons drawn and their expressions set with grim determination. "End of the line, Mr. Turbo," Alvarez said, his voice laced with triumph. "You put up a good fight, I'll give you that. But in the end, you were no match for me."

Turbo felt a sense of hopelessness wash over him as he realized that he was trapped. He had come so close to escaping, only to have his freedom snatched away at the last moment.

As the guards moved in to apprehend him, Turbo knew that he had to try one last, desperate gambit. With a surge of adrenaline, he lunged forward, knocking one of the guards off his feet and sending the man tumbling over the edge of the loading dock.

The sound of the guard's agonized scream as he fell sent a chill down Turbo's spine, but he didn't have time to dwell

on it. He had to keep moving, had to find a way to escape before Alvarez and his men caught up with him.

Sprinting towards the van, Turbo yanked open the driver's side door, his heart pounding in his chest. If he could just get the vehicle started, he might have a chance of making a clean getaway.

But as he slid behind the wheel, he felt a sudden, sharp pain in his back, and he knew that he had been hit. Turbo let out a strangled cry, his vision blurring as he desperately tried to start the engine. The sound of Alvarez's laughter filled the air, and Turbo knew that his time was up. He had given it his all, but in the end, he had been no match for the ruthless criminal mastermind.

As his strength began to fade, Turbo felt a sense of resignation wash over him. He had failed, failed to find Hector, failed to expose Alvarez's twisted operation,

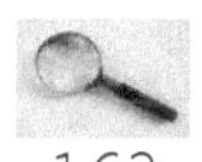

and now he was going to pay the ultimate price.

Closing his eyes, Turbo braced himself for the end, his mind filled with thoughts of Maria and her children, and the promise he had made to them. He had let them down, and he knew that they would never know the truth about what had happened to Hector.

But just as Turbo was about to succumb to the darkness, a sudden sound caught his attention. It was the faint sound of sirens in the distance, growing steadily louder with each passing moment.

Turbo's eyes snapped open, a glimmer of hope igniting within him. Could it be that someone had discovered his predicament and called the authorities? Or was it just a cruel trick of fate, taunting him with the prospect of rescue only to snatch it away at the last moment?

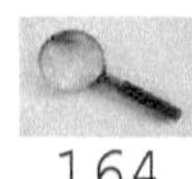

Alvarez seemed to sense the change in Turbo's demeanor, and his expression darkened. "What's the matter, Turbo?" he sneered, his voice dripping with contempt. "Not ready to give up just yet?"

Turbo summoned what little strength he had left, his voice barely above a whisper. "It's over, Alvarez. The police are coming, and this time, there's no escaping them."

Alvarez's eyes narrowed, and for a moment, Turbo thought he saw a flicker of fear in the man's expression. But it was quickly replaced by a cold, calculating look, and Turbo knew that Alvarez was not about to go down without a fight.

"We'll see about that, Turbo," Alvarez said, his voice laced with menace. "I've got more tricks up my sleeve than you can imagine."

With that, Alvarez turned and barked a series of orders to his men, his expression set with grim determination. Turbo watched as the guards sprang into action, securing the perimeter and preparing to make their escape.

As the sirens grew closer, Turbo felt a surge of hope rise within him. This was his chance, his one opportunity to bring Alvarez down and expose the truth about his twisted operation. He had to find a way to hold out, to stall for time until the authorities arrived.

Gritting his teeth against the pain, Turbo forced himself to sit upright, his eyes locked on Alvarez. "You won't get away with this, Alvarez," he said, his voice steadier than he had expected. "The police are coming, and they're not going to stop until they bring you and your entire operation down."

Alvarez let out a cold laugh, his eyes gleaming with malice. "Oh, I think you'll find that I have a few surprises in store for the police, Turbo. And when this is all over, you'll be nothing more than a distant memory."

Turbo felt a chill run down his spine as he realized the full extent of Alvarez's power and influence. This was a man who was not to be trifled with, a man who had built an empire on the backs of the most vulnerable members of society.

As the sound of the sirens grew closer, Turbo knew that he had to take a risk, to do whatever it took to bring Alvarez down. He had come too far to give up now, and he refused to let the man's twisted scheme succeed.

Summoning every ounce of strength he had left, Turbo lunged forward, his hands reaching for Alvarez's throat. The guards immediately sprang into action, but Turbo

refused to back down, his grip tightening around Alvarez's neck.

Alvarez let out a choked gasp, his eyes widening with a mixture of surprise and fury. "You fool!" he snarled, his voice barely above a whisper. "You'll only make things worse for yourself!"

Turbo felt a surge of triumph rise within him, but it was short-lived. Suddenly, he felt a sharp pain in his side, and he let out a strangled cry, his grip on Alvarez's throat slipping.

As he crumpled to the ground, Turbo caught a glimpse of one of the guards, his weapon still smoking. He had been shot, and this time, the wound was serious.

Alvarez towered over him, his expression a mix of triumph and contempt. "I told you, Turbo," he hissed. "You're no match for me."

Turbo felt the world around him begin to fade, his vision blurring as the pain overwhelmed him. He had failed, failed to bring Alvarez to justice, failed to protect Hector's family, failed in everything he had set out to do.

As the sound of the sirens grew deafening, Turbo summoned the last of his strength to whisper a single word: "Maria..."

And then, everything went dark.

The phone rang in Pablo's office and it was Lt. Jameson from the police. He informed Pablo that Turbo had been shot 3 times and was in critical condition in Beverly hospital in Montebello. Pablo then rushed to turbo's side. There was nothing that Pablo could do but wait.

After several hours Turbo was out of surgery. The Doctor informed Pablo that bullet in his back had missed his spine by ½ inch. Turbo would make a full

recovery after couple months of rehabilitation. Pablo waited at the hospital until he could see and talk to Turbo.

After several more hours Pablo was allowed to visit Turbo. Pablo, with a worried look on his face, "How are you feeling, buddy, Are you in pain? Turbo replied "I feel a little drowsy. Did the doctor tell you about my condition? Will I walk again?". "Of course, nobody can take you out of the game that easy but you will be sidelined for a couple of months". "Did you capture Alvarez?". Pablo indicated that Alvarez got away but that he would do everything he could to track him down.

Turbo, after much silence, told Pablo to call Frank. Frank would be a good resource in the effort to being Alvarez and his gang to justice.

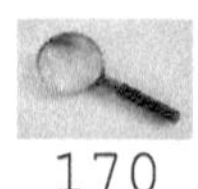

Maria sat at her kitchen table her eyes red from crying. It had been weeks since Hector had disappeared, and the police had made no progress in their investigation.

She got a call from Pablo telling her that Turbo was severely wounded and was in the hospital. And Hector, her beloved Hector, was still missing.

Maria felt a wave of despair wash over her, and she buried her face in her hands, her body shaking with sobs. She had put her trust in Turbo, had believed that he could help her find Hector and bring him home.

As the reality of the situation sank in, Maria felt a surge of anger rise within her. She would find a way to uncover the truth, to expose the man responsible for her husband's disappearance.

Pablo felt a steely determination take hold. He was going to find out what

happened to Hector, no matter what it took. And he was going to make sure that Turbo's shooting and injuries were not in vain.

Arriving at the office, Pablo set to work, his mind racing with a thousand different ideas and strategies. He knew that she couldn't do this alone, that he was going to need help if he was going to uncover the truth.

Reaching for the phone, Pablo dialed the number of the only person he could trust – Turbo's old friend and confidante, a former cop named Frank. He had met him a few times during the course of Turbo's investigation, and he knew that he was the only one who might be able to help him now.

"Frank? This is Pablo, Turbo's Partner. I need your help."

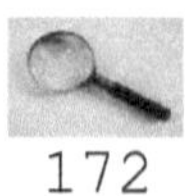

There was a moment of silence, and then Frank's voice, laced with concern. "Pablo? What's happened?"

"Turbo is in Beverly hospital. He was shot 3 times but he will fully recover. I need to find Hector".

He heard Frank suck in a sharp breath, and he could almost see the shock and sadness on his face. "Dammit," he muttered, his voice low and gravelly. "I knew that stubborn bastard was getting in over his head."

"Frank, I need your help. The police aren't doing enough, and I can't let Hector's disappearance and Turbo's shooting go unsolved. Will you help me?"

There was another brief pause, and then Frank's voice, resolute and determined. "Of course, Pablo. I'll be there as soon as I can."

With Frank's help, Pablo was going to get to the bottom of this, no matter what it

took. He was going to find Hector, and he was going to make sure that Turbo's shooting would be solved.

The next few days were a whirlwind of activity. Frank arrived at Pablo's office, his brow furrowed with concern and determination. Together, they set to work, scouring every inch of the investigation that Turbo had conducted, searching for any clues or leads that could point them in the right direction. It was slow and painstaking work, but Pablo refused to give up. He knew that the answers were out there, hidden somewhere in the tangled web of lies and corruption that had led to Hector's disappearance and Turbo's shooting.

As they dug deeper, Pablo and Frank began to uncover a disturbing pattern. It seemed that Hector's disappearance was connected to a larger, more sinister

operation - one that involved human trafficking and organized crime.

The more they uncovered, the more Pablo's heart sank. He had always known that the streets of East LA were a dangerous place, but he had never imagined the depths of the corruption and depravity that lurked beneath the surface.

And as they pieced together the evidence, a terrifying realization dawned on them - Hector had not simply disappeared, but had been targeted, abducted, and likely taken to be sold as part of this twisted criminal enterprise.

Frank, too, was equally resolute. He had known Turbo for years, and the private eye's shooting had hit him hard. But he was determined to get revenge for his friend by ensuring that the truth was uncovered and that the individuals responsible were brought to justice.

Together, Pablo and Frank began to formulate a plan, drawing on Frank's connections and experience as a former cop to try and infiltrate the criminal network that they had uncovered. It was a dangerous, high-stakes game, but they knew that they had no other choice.

As they delved deeper into the investigation, they began to uncover even more disturbing details. It seemed that the human trafficking operation they were up against was far-reaching and well-entrenched, with connections that stretched all the way to the highest levels of power.

The deeper they dug, the more they realized just how dangerous their mission had become. They were up against a formidable adversary, one that was willing to do whatever it took to protect its twisted empire.

But even in the face of these
overwhelming odds, Pablo and Frank
refused to back down. They were driven by
a fierce determination to bring Hector
home, and to ensure that Turbo's injuries
were not in vain.

As they continued their investigation,
they encountered numerous obstacles and
setbacks, each one threatening to derail
their efforts. But they persevered,
driven by an unwavering sense of purpose
and a deep sense of personal investment
in the case.

Finally, after weeks of painstaking work
and countless dead ends, they caught a
break. A tip from one of Frank's old
contacts led them to a suspected
trafficking hub, a nondescript warehouse
on the outskirts of the city.

With their hearts pounding in their
chests, Pablo and Frank made their way to
the warehouse, praying that this lead

would finally lead them to Hector. They knew that they were venturing into dangerous territory, but they were determined to see this through, no matter the cost.

As they approached the warehouse, they could feel the tension in the air, a palpable sense of danger that made the hairs on the back of their necks stand on end. But they pressed on, steeling themselves for whatever might lie ahead. Cautiously, they made their way inside, their eyes scanning the dimly lit interior for any sign of Hector or the traffickers they were after. The warehouse was eerily silent, save for the faint sound of movement in the distance. Exchanging a tense glance, Pablo and Frank pressed forward, their footsteps echoing in the cavernous space. They knew that they were walking a razor's edge,

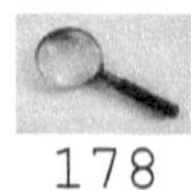

that one wrong move could mean the end
for them both.

Suddenly, a voice rang out, cutting
through the silence like a knife.

"Well, well, what do we have here?"

Pablo and Frank whirled around, their
hearts pounding, to see a figure emerge
from the shadows, a sinister smile
playing on his lips.

"Alvarez," Frank growled, his hand
instinctively moving towards his
holster.

The man, Alvarez, let out a cold laugh.
"I had a feeling you two might show up.
You've been poking your noses where they
don't belong."

Pablo felt a surge of fear, but she
refused to back down. "Where's Hector?"
he demanded. Alvarez's smile widened, and
he shook his head in mock sympathy. "I'm
afraid Hector is long gone. He's been a
valuable asset in my little operation."

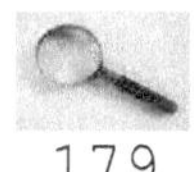

Alvarez chuckled his eyes gleaming with malice. "Oh, don't worry, he's in good hands. After all, there's a high demand for exotic merchandise these days."

Frank stepped forward, his face a mask of rage. "You're going to pay for this, Alvarez. For Hector, for Turbo, and for everyone else you've hurt."

Alvarez's expression darkened, and he raised a hand, signaling to the shadows. "I don't think so, my friend. You see, I've got a few friends of my own who are eager to meet you."

Suddenly, the warehouse erupted into chaos as a group of armed men emerged from the darkness, their weapons trained on Pablo and Frank. The two of them were hopelessly outnumbered, and they knew that their only chance was to find a way to escape.

As the men closed in, Pablo felt a surge of desperation rise within him.

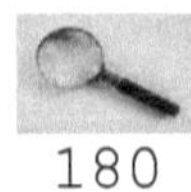

With a burst of adrenaline, he lunged forward, knocking one of the men to the ground. Frank, too, sprang into action, his fists flying as he fought to create an opening for them to escape.

But Alvarez was not about to let them go so easily. He barked orders to his men, his voice laced with fury, and the battle intensified.

Pablo and Frank fought with everything they had, but they were outmatched and outgunned. As the minutes ticked by, they began to feel their strength waning, their bodies battered and bruised.

Just when it seemed that all hope was lost, a sudden sound caught their attention - the wail of sirens in the distance. Pablo felt a surge of hope rise within him, and he redoubled his efforts, his eyes fixed on the distant lights.

Alvarez, too, seemed to realize the gravity of the situation, and his

expression darkened with a mix of fear and fury. He shouted orders to his men, his voice laced with desperation, and they began to scatter, their weapons still trained on Pablo and Frank.

As the sirens grew closer, Alvarez turned to Pablo, his eyes narrowed with hatred. "This isn't over," he yelled, before turning and fleeing into the shadows.

Pablo and Frank watched as the men disappeared, their hearts pounding with a mixture of relief and dread. They had come so close to uncovering the truth, to finding Hector, and now they were left with more questions than answers.

As the police swarmed the warehouse, Pablo felt a surge of exhaustion wash over him. He had put everything he had into this, and he couldn't bear the thought of failing Hector and Turbo.

But as the officers surrounded them, Pablo knew that they had no choice but to

trust in the system, to let the authorities take over and try to uncover the truth.

As the police officers began to question them, Pablo and Frank knew that they were facing an uphill battle. The odds were stacked against them, and the enemy they were up against was powerful and ruthless.

But they also knew that they had no choice but to keep fighting. For Hector, for Turbo, and for the countless others who had been trapped in Alvarez's twisted web of deceit and exploitation.

As Pablo and Frank were interrogated by the police, they knew that they were walking a fine line. They couldn't risk revealing too much about their own investigation, especially since it had led them into such dangerous territory.

The detectives were skeptical at first, questioning the validity of their claims

and the reliability of their sources. But as Pablo and Frank continued to provide detailed information about Alvarez's criminal operation, the officers began to take them more seriously.

"So, let me get this straight," one of the detectives said, his brow furrowed in concentration. "You're telling us that this Alvarez character is running a massive human trafficking ring, with connections that go all the way to the top?"

Pablo nodded her expressive grin. "That's right. Hector was targeted, abducted, and is now being held as part of this twisted operation. And Turbo's injuries were devastating.

Frank spoke up, his voice gruff but determined. "Look, you've got to believe us. Alvarez is a dangerous man, and he's not going to stop until he's got what he wants. We need to take him down, and we

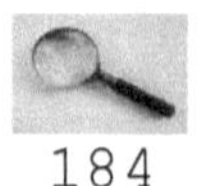

need to find Hector before it's too late."

The detective considered their words, his expression thoughtful. "Alright, I'll level with you. We've been investigating Alvarez for a while now, but we've never been able to pin anything concrete on him. This information you've provided could be a real game-changer."

Pablo felt a glimmer of hope rise within him. "So you're going to help us?"

The detective nodded. "We'll do everything we can. But I need you two to work with us, to share everything you know. We can't take Alvarez down alone, and we can't risk any more lives in the process."

Pablo and Frank exchanged a glance, both of them well aware of the risks involved. But they also knew that they had no other choice.

"Alright," Pablo said, his voice steady. "We'll help you, but we're coming with you.

The detective hesitated his expression conflicted. "I understand but this is a dangerous operation. I can't guarantee your safety."

Frank stepped forward, his eyes narrowing. "Look, detective, we've been in this thing from the start. We know the risks, and we're not backing down. Hector's life is on the line, and we're not leaving it in your hands alone."

The detective let out a heavy sigh, realizing that he wasn't going to be able to dissuade them. "Alright, fine. But you follow our lead, and you do exactly what we tell you to, understand?"

Pablo and Frank nodded their expressions resolute. They knew that they were taking a huge risk, but they also knew that they had no other choice. Hector's life

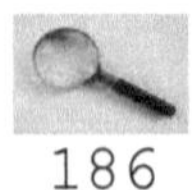

depended on them, and they weren't about to let him down.

As the police began to mobilize, Pablo and Frank found themselves swept up in the flurry of activity. They were briefed on the plan, their roles and responsibilities clearly laid out. It was a high-stakes operation, and they knew that there was no room for error.

As they made their way to the warehouse, Pablo felt a sense of dread and determination wash over him.

When they arrived, the warehouse was swarming with officers, all of them poised and ready to move in. Pablo and Frank were instructed to stay back, to provide support and intelligence as needed.

As the raid began, Pablo felt his heart pounding in his chest. He watched tensely as the officers stormed the building,

their weapons drawn and their faces set with grim determination.

The sound of gunfire echoed through the air.

Finally, after what felt like an eternity, the officers emerged, their expressions a mix of triumph and sorrow. The detective who had questioned them earlier approached his face grim. "Alvarez got away," he said, his voice laced with frustration. "We found some of his men, but the bastard himself slipped through our fingers."

Pablo felt a wave of despair wash over him. "And Hector? Did you find him?"

The detective shook his head, his expression apologetic. "I'm sorry. We searched the entire warehouse, but there's no sign of Hector. It looks like Alvarez managed to get him out before we arrived."

The detective cleared his throat, his expression somber. "We're going to keep searching. We won't rest until we've tracked down Alvarez and rescued Hector. But I have to warn you, the odds aren't looking good."
Alvarez is a slippery bastard, and we're going to need all the intel we can get if we're going to track him down."
As the investigation continued, Pablo and Frank found themselves working closely with the police, providing them with every bit of information they had uncovered about Alvarez's operation. They knew that time was of the essence, and they couldn't afford to let any leads slip through their fingers.
But even as they worked tirelessly, the weight of the situation began to take its toll.
The days turned into weeks, and the search for Hector only seemed to grow

more and more fruitless. The police
followed every lead, raided every
suspected trafficking hub, but they
always seemed to be one step behind
Alvarez.

Frank was feeling the strain. He had
known Turbo for years, and the private
eye's severe injuries had hit him hard.
But he refused to let Turbo's shooting be
in vain, and he was determined to see
this thing through to the end.

One night, as Pablo sat alone in the
office a sudden realization dawned on
him. He couldn't keep relying on the
police, on their limited resources and
their bureaucratic red tape. If he was
going to find Hector, he was going to
have to take matters into his own hands.
Without hesitating, he reached for the
phone, dialing Frank's number with a
sense of renewed purpose. When he

answered, Pablo could hear the exhaustion in Frank's voice.

"Frank, I need your help," he said, his voice steady and resolute. "We've been going about this all wrong. It's time to take the fight to Alvarez."

Frank was silent for a moment, and Pablo could almost see the wheels turning in his mind. "What are you thinking, Pablo?" he asked, his voice heavy with trepidation.

"I'm thinking we need to go rogue," Pablo replied, his eyes gleaming with a dangerous edge. "We've been playing by the rules, and it's gotten us nowhere. It's time to take the gloves off and do whatever it takes to bring Hector home."

Frank let out a heavy sigh, but Pablo could hear the hint of reluctant agreement in his voice. "I don't like it, Pablo. It's dangerous, and it could jeopardize the entire investigation."

"I don't care, Frank," Pablo shot back, his voice laced with desperation. "Hector is running out of time, and I'm not going to let him down. We have to do this, no matter what the cost."

There was a long pause on the other end of the line, and Pablo held his breath, waiting for Frank's response. Finally, he heard him let out a resigned sigh.

"Alright, Pablo. I'm in. But we need to be careful, and we need to have a plan. This is a dangerous game we're playing."

Pablo felt a surge of relief and determination wash over him. "I understand, Frank. But I promise you, we're going to bring Hector home. No matter what it takes."

With that, Pablo and Frank began to formulate their plan, their minds racing with a thousand different scenarios and contingencies. They knew that they were venturing into uncharted territory, but

they also knew that they had no other choice.

As they worked, Pablo couldn't help but feel a sense of dread and fear. He was risking everything, putting his own life on the line in the hopes of rescuing Hector. But he knew that he couldn't live with herself if he didn't at least try.

Finally, after days of meticulous planning and preparation, Pablo and Frank were ready to put their plan into action. They had gathered a small, trusted team of allies, people who were as determined as they were to bring down Alvarez and his twisted operation.

With a deep breath, they set out, their hearts pounding in their chests. They knew that they were up against a formidable enemy, one who would stop at nothing to protect his empire. But they also knew that they had no other choice.

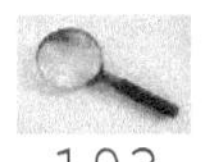

As they made their way to the latest suspected trafficking hub, Pablo felt a sense of dread and anticipation wash over him. This was it, the moment of truth. They were either going to succeed in rescuing Hector, or they were going to fail, and the consequences would be unimaginable.

But as they approached the nondescript warehouse, Pablo felt a surge of determination rise within him. He was going to do whatever it took to bring Hector home, no matter the cost.

Signaling to his team, Pablo and Frank moved in, their weapons drawn and their senses on high alert. They knew that they were outnumbered and outgunned, but they also knew that they had the element of surprise on their side.

The sound of gunfire erupted, echoing through the night air, and Pablo felt his heart pounding in his chest. He knew that

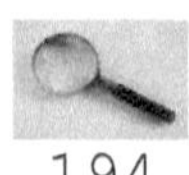

they were in the fight of their lives, but he refused to back down.

As the battle raged on, Pablo caught a glimpse of a familiar figure in the distance, and his breath caught in his throat. It was Hector, his eyes wild with fear and desperation, as he was dragged away by a group of armed men.

Without hesitating, Pablo broke free from the chaos, his eyes locked on Hector's retreating form. He had come too far to give up now, and he wasn't about to let Hector slip through her fingers.

Ignoring the hail of bullets that whizzed past him, Pablo charged forward, his legs pumping with a desperate urgency. He had to reach Hector, had to save him from the nightmare that he had been trapped in for so long.

As he drew closer, he could see the fear and relief in Hector's eyes, and he felt a surge of hope rise within. They were so

close, so close to finally putting an end
to this nightmare.

But just as he reached out to him, a
gunshot rang out, and Pablo felt a
searing pain in his side. He stumbled,
his vision blurring, as he realized that
he had been hit.

Hector let out an anguished cry, his eyes
wide with terror, and Pablo knew that he
had to keep going, no matter the cost. He
had to get him to safety, had to protect
him at all costs.

With the last of his strength, Pablo
lunged forward, wrapping his arms around
Hector and shielding him from the barrage
of gunfire. He could feel the warmth of
his body, the rapid beating of his heart,
and he knew that he had to hold on, no
matter what.

As the world around him faded to black,
Pablo felt a sense of peace wash over
him. He had done it, he had kept his

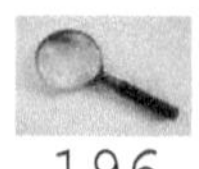

promise to Turbo, to bring Hector home. And even if he didn't make it, he knew that Hector was safe.

The sound of sirens in the distance, the shouts and cries of his team, all faded into the background as Pablo succumbed to the darkness, his last thoughts a whispered prayer for Hector's safety.

The world around Pablo was a blur of chaos and confusion as the sound of sirens filled the air. He could hear the shouts and cries of his team, the thunderous crack of gunfire, but his focus was solely on Hector.

But as the darkness began to creep in, Pablo couldn't help but feel a twinge of regret. He had come so far, overcome so many obstacles, only to fall at the final hurdle. He had wanted so desperately to see Hector's safe return.

But now, as the world faded around him, Pablo knew that his time had run out. He

could feel the warmth of Hector's body against his, the rapid beating of his heart, and he prayed that he would be able to escape this nightmare, that he would be able to rebuild his life.

The sound of the sirens grew louder, and Pablo could hear the thunderous approach of more vehicles. Help was coming, but he knew that it might be too late for him.

As the darkness enveloped him, Pablo felt a sense of relief wash over him. He had done all that he could, and now it was up to Hector, to Frank, and to the authorities to finish what Turbo had started. He knew that they would stop at nothing to bring down Alvarez and his twisted operation, and he took solace in that knowledge.

When Pablo opened his eyes, he found himself in a sterile, unfamiliar environment. The beeping of machines and the sharp scent of antiseptic told him

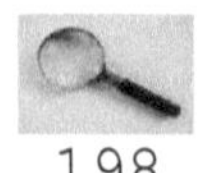

that he was in a hospital, but the details of how he had arrived there were a blur.

As he struggled to regain his bearings, a familiar face came into focus - Frank, his eyes red-rimmed and his expression a mix of relief and concern. Turbo was also alongside Pablo's bed.

"Pablo," he breathed, reaching out to grasp his hand. "Thank God you're awake."

Pablo blinked, his mind racing to piece together the fragments of his memory.

Turbo was relieved that Pablo would be O.K. "I was worried that you and Frank might get into something that you couldn't get out of".

"Hector," Pablo croaked, his voice raspy with disuse. "Where's Hector?"

Frank's expression darkened, and Pablo felt his heart sink. "The police found him," he said quietly. "They... they got him out, but he's not in good shape."

"He's alive, Pablo. But it's going to be a long road to recovery. The things they did to him..." his voice trailed off, unable to finish the sentence.

As Frank left to make the necessary arrangements, Pablo took a moment to gather his thoughts. He knew that the road ahead would be long and arduous, but he was ready to face it head-on. Hector was alive, and that was all that mattered.

Over the next few hours, Frank recounted the details of Hector's ordeal, painting a horrific picture of the abuse and suffering he had endured at the hands of Alvarez's men.

By the time Frank had finished, Pablo was trembling with a mixture of grief and rage. He had known that Hector's captivity had been a nightmare, but the reality was far worse than he could have imagined.

"We have to make them pay, Frank," he said, his voice low and fierce. "Alvarez and his entire organization, they have to be brought down. I won't rest until they're all behind bars."

Frank nodded his expression grim. "I know, Pablo. And we're going to do everything in our power to make that happen. The police are already building their case, and they're determined to bring Alvarez and his men to justice."

Alvarez was a powerful and influential man, with connections that reached deep into the heart of the city's power structure. Taking him down would be no easy feat.

Frank and the police continued their investigation, piecing together the evidence that would bring Alvarez and his organization to its knees. They worked tirelessly, following every lead and leaving no stone unturned, driven by a

shared determination to see justice served.

And as the investigation progressed, Pablo and Frank began to uncover even more disturbing revelations about the depth and breadth of Alvarez's criminal enterprise. It was a sprawling, multi-layered operation that extended far beyond the borders of East LA, with tentacles that reached into the highest echelons of power.

The task ahead of them seemed daunting, but Pablo refused to be daunted. He had come too far, endured too much, to turn back now. Hector's safety and the safety of countless others depended on their success, and he was determined to see it through to the bitter end.

As the weeks turned into months, Pablo and Frank continued to work tirelessly, their partnership forged in the crucible of the trauma they had both endured. They

were a formidable team, driven by a shared sense of purpose and a refusal to be cowed by the overwhelming odds they faced.

And as the investigation took unexpected turns and new leads emerged, they began to uncover the full scope of Alvarez's ambitions. It became clear that his criminal empire was not just a local operation, but rather a global network of human trafficking and exploitation, with tentacles that stretched across continents.

The task of taking down such a vast and deeply entrenched organization seemed almost impossible, but Pablo and Frank refused to be deterred. They knew that the fate of countless lives hung in the balance, and they were determined to see this through, no matter the cost.

Politicians, law enforcement officials, and even members of the judiciary had all

been compromised by Alvarez's vast network of influence and intimidation.

In the end, it was a long and arduous battle, one that tested their every ounce of strength and resilience. But as the final pieces of the puzzle began to fall into place, Pablo and Frank knew that they were closer than ever to bringing Alvarez and his entire criminal empire crashing down.

The moment of reckoning came in a carefully orchestrated sting operation, with law enforcement agencies from around the world converging on Alvarez's headquarters in a coordinated strike. The battle was fierce and bloody, but in the end, justice prevailed.

As Alvarez and his lieutenants were taken into custody, Pablo felt a wave of relief and triumph wash over him. He went through all of this for Turbo, the real hero in the effort to capture and destroy

the Alvarez corrupt empire. It was over, the nightmare was finally at an end. Hector was safe, and the men who had tormented him and so many others were finally facing the consequences of their actions.

In the aftermath, Pablo, Frank, and Turbo were hailed as heroes, their tireless efforts and unwavering dedication to the cause celebrated by all who had been touched by Alvarez's twisted crimes.

Follow Turbo and Pablo in their continuing story of solving interesting and complex cases in "Turbo and Pablo – Private Investigators in East Los Angeles in the 1980's".

My Other Works Include:
The Robin Hood Virus

The Robin Hood Virus – Discovery

The Robin Hood Virus – Validation

Worldwide Trivia from the 1930's including Military Trivia Book 1

Worldwide Trivia from the 1930's including Military Trivia Book 2

Worldwide Trivia from the 1930's including Military Trivia Book 3

A Riverboat Odyssey

A Riverboat Odyssey – Astrid's Final Journey

Turbo – A Private Detective in East Los Angeles during the 1960's

Turbo – A Private Detective in East Los Angeles during the 1970's

Turbo – A Private Detective in East Los Angeles during the 1980's

9 79982 249913 89